THE

FINGERPRINT

KILLER

Author: Alex Blank

Published by

World Wide Unique Media

In cooperation with

Information Publishing

Meriden, Connecticut. USA 06450

ISBN: 978-0-9826929-1-2

Printed in the United States of America

Special thanks to Joey W. for cover pictures of Alektra Blue.

Axel's Prelude

Even if it's just buried deep in their subconscious, some serial killers want to get caught. I never understood why. They leave clues and patterns like some deranged riddler from a comic book. I get that they think they're accomplishing something; I get that they think their work is art to share with the world; and I get that they think they must be brilliant to stay several steps in front of the cops. So, on some level, they crave the acknowledgement… I am not one of those. I don't need the credit or the glory. My satisfaction comes from the kill itself, not having admirers. That's why I make sure my work doesn't leave a pattern, and the cops never suspect my victims are all taken by the same person. If they don't have reason to believe a serial killer exists, they won't be looking for one.

I'm partial to cutting, particularly throats, but I mix it up. Again, this is to make sure the cops never see a pattern, and that way, I can just leave the body at the scene. Sometimes I leave her undamaged except her throat, and sometimes I completely mutilate her. Sometimes I leave her throat untouched, and get creative.

I have unregistered guns, but have only killed with a gun once before – too much noise, and not nearly as personal or satisfying. But whenever I'm far enough away, in distance or time, from my last throat cutting, that's my preference. I never use the same knife twice so that the wounds don't give me away either. The details are the difference between freedom and lethal injection.

Picking a victim is important. She has to have a certain je ne sais quoi, and then circumstance has to present opportunity. Hookers and call girls are easy prey, but when going that route, I vary locations where I find them. And just because a woman takes money for sex, doesn't mean the cops are aware this is her profession.

I don't return to the scene of the crime and ask questions or pretend to try to help the police. Best case is you get a little info about a crime you already know everything about. Maybe you feel superior to the bumbling idiots while you boldly stand in front of them, hiding in plain sight, as they're searching for you. But worst case is they notice your interest and take a close look at you. I don't need that.

More common sense stuff: I don't park illegally when I'm about to kill – how retarded is that? I don't buy gas or anything close to the crime scene with a credit card. This in itself may not be incriminating, but why place myself in the area? I don't leave calling cards like a rose or a puzzle piece stuffed in a victim's ass. And I don't take NOTICABLE trophies, like jewelry or ....teeth.

But I do like a souvenir. I take fingerprints. In the old days, I would just use plain white paper. But years ago, I started using the actual paper that cops use - the kind with a section for each specific finger, lined out. And I keep an instant camera for 'before death' and 'after death' pictures. The fingerprints are somewhat of a compulsion that feels like building a collection, which is satisfying in itself. But the pictures bring back specific memories and are sexually gratifying to me.

I have no reservations about keeping these items. Nothing is missing at the crime scene, so nothing appears to have been taken. Each murder seems completely unrelated to my others. And since I don't know any of my victims personally, their friends and families and acquaintances have never seen me. So, there's never a motive for me to be a suspect. As long as I avoid suspicion, there's no reason the cops will want to search my home, so they'll never find this collection.

I know I'll never get caught. But one day, after I've died of old age, someone will be cleaning out my place and find these fingerprints and the pictures... and the world will know of my hobby. I expect my name will live on, long after I'm gone. That's a satisfying feeling, but I still have no desire to be famous now. I like freedom, and I like being alive.

My name is Axel Simmons. I'm white. I'm 37. I'm a locksmith - a skill that comes in very handy...

<u>Several months in the future:</u>

Axel has a knife through his right temple and it's penetrating several inches into his brain. A woman he thought was dead has just stabbed him. He collapses onto the bathroom floor and has a seizure, but he doesn't die. As he recovers from the seizure, the woman is gone, and Axel is relieved to discover that he still has a penis…

Chapter 1
Mexican Cravings / Vicky Enters

Axel lives in Los Angeles, but this evening he's taken a road trip to Tijuana. He's procured a motel room, and as expected, with a little extra cash, no ID required. It's a small dirty room with one bed, a desk and chair, and a small filthy bathroom. But the only concern Axel has is that he can virtually hear his neighbors breathing in the room next door; he knows he'll have to be near silent tonight. But he's far enough from home to be confident that police working this case won't connect his previous victims, and his future victims, to tonight's festivities.

Axel opens his travel bag and stashes a dagger between the box spring and the mattress on the right side of the bed. The dagger is long and skinny. The blade is about 6 inches long, has blades on both sides, and comes to a very sharp point at the tip. Axel goes looking for that special someone.

Axel doesn't have to walk very long before a local man is telling him, "The finest women in all of Mexico are just inside this door." It's a seedy strip club and as good of a prospect as anywhere, so the $5.00 cover seems like a bargain.

Upon entering, however, it's not a pretty sight … this is NOT Mexico's finest women. The woman currently on stage is at least

50 years old, and though she does have very large tits, they are swinging at about her belly button. Another of these 'strippers,' carrying a drink tray between sets, is at least 40 pounds over-weight; and though they are healed, she has more knife wounds on her body than Axel's last two victims combined. He starts to head back out, and a moderately more attractive woman approaches with, what must be, her pimp. "Do ya wanna have sex with my seeester for $40.00?" he asks. But before Axel can answer, she flashes a smile. Her teeth, all 5 of them, were a shade between yellow and green and black. And he could smell her breath as she smiled, which was a cross between a tequila worm left rotting in the sun for a day, and water used in a bong for a week after it was used to boil hot dogs for a month. This was completely unacceptable. So, it's back onto the street to look for someone pleasant enough to kill.

Axel asks the man who flagged him into the joint if he knows where he can really find some grade-A women (and hands him a twenty). He tells Axel, "If you got a couple hundred dollars, go to the club on the next block and tell the bouncer that Jose told you to ask for Pedro… But if you want a REALLY unforgettable evening, I can get you into the donkey show at my cousin's farm."

Axel heads to the club to see Pedro. Halfway there, two rather hot American party girls, one blonde and one brunette, are staggering the opposite way down the street towards Axel. As they cross paths, the blonde engages Axel - as if they might want to hookup. "Hey cutie, wanna party with us?" holding her beer wildly in the air. These girls are very young (and very pretty) to be approaching Axel, and he's flattered and intrigued for a moment. His game plan was for Mexican this evening, but spontaneity could also be part of the thrill. But a second later, the blonde hurls uncontrollably, and she hurls in Axel's general direction. Axel has to jump back to avoid the vomit, but a little ricochets off the ground and onto his left shoe. Though he felt like killing her just for this, his prey must be conscious and lucid. Killing a sedated girl to Axel would be like fucking a dead girl for a normal guy.

At the club, Axel approaches the bouncer, "Jose sent me… I'm looking for Pedro." Axel is sent into the club where the music is blaring. It's the kind of dance music that's thumping and mind numbing. He proceeds through a narrow hallway and into a large room where only muffled traces of the thumping can get to. A fat Mexican man is sitting at a desk with two, what must be, bodyguards behind him. There are about a dozen women scattered about the rest of the room behind the men. Most are average at best, but a few are good-looking. There are some particularly young girls there, probably as young as 14, but Axel isn't a pedophile.

Pedro says, "You pay $200.00 and you get your pick. For $150.00… I pick. You get one of the rooms above for 30 minutes. If you want multiple girls, we can talk... You get disrespectful with the girls or you fuck with me, and we'll tea-bag you with your own balls!"

Axel replies, "How much to take that one out of this shit-hole and keep her 'til morning?" He points to the one true stand-out of the lot. She's a young pretty Mexican woman who's been making eye contact with Axel, clearly wanting this customer. Maria looks to be about 20. She's about 5'5'' with long dark hair and olive-skinned complexion. She's very thin and her breasts look to be about a B-cup.

Pedro summons, "Maria, get over here … you wanna go off site, overnight for this one?" She answers, "Sure, why not?" Pedro offers, "Give me $700.00 now and pay Maria $300.00 in the morning."

Axel pays the $700.00, but realizes he made a mistake going direct to the pimp. Usually he can offer a prostitute any amount of money and never actually have to pay it. Or he can re-claim it after her untimely passing.

They walk to Axel's motel room. It's getting late, about 1:00 am. There's no sound coming from the neighbors rooms, so they're either asleep or out. Axel offers Maria a drink as he pulls out a bottle of tequila from his suitcase. They both take a swig from the bottle. Axel then pulls out his camera, "You are so beautiful. Can I take your picture to remember you by?" Maria smiles and lifts some of her hair with her hands to pose as Axel pushes the button. The picture slides out of the instant camera.

Axel takes off his shirt and lies on the bed with his back up against the wall. Maria slides off all of her clothes and approaches Axel on the bed so that she's lying face down between Axel's legs. She undoes his belt and pants, and takes his penis in her mouth. She looks up to his face looking for approval as she performs. Axel says, "You're doing good... Don't look up at me."

Axel's left hand is dangling over the edge of the bed... not far from his dagger. He's considering reaching for it and driving the blade through the back of her neck as she's blowing him. Since she's not looking at his face, he's free to just stare at the back of her neck. He brushes her hair to the sides. This exposed vulnerable target has him aroused much more than the superlative blowjob he's receiving.

All of a sudden Axel feels off balance and dizzy. He grips the bed's covers tight in each hand to brace himself. It only lasts a few seconds. This has never happened to him before. Maria doesn't notice anything is wrong; she probably thinks the reaction is due to her efforts. Axel shakes it off and is right back in the moment staring at her sexy delicate neck. He can feel his climax building and whispers, "Don't look up ... Swallow it and I'll pay you double." Maria speeds up a little and never looks up.

In one fast motion, Axel grabs the dagger with his left hand, braces the top of Maria's head with his right hand, withdraws his dick from her throat to a shallower depth in her mouth, and thrusts the dagger, point first through the nape of her neck.

It sinks all the way through her neck and pokes through the front of her throat, and the tip rips into the bed covers a little. It was quite an adrenaline rush to get the blade to penetrate so far. Axel doesn't know exactly how deep in her throat his dick had been in reference to the back of her neck, but he has a sudden sense of relief that he thought to withdraw some. He ponders the nightmarish scenario of himself stuck in her mouth, with the dagger going through the back of her neck, skewering through his penis and out the front of her throat. That would be one to add to the world's stupidest criminals stories for sure.

Now, for a moment, everything is still and quiet, and a feeling of tranquility and peace washes over Axel. He takes a deep breath and soaks it up. He gets up, fixes his pants and belt, and grabs his camera. Maria is face down in the middle of the bed, motionless … dead. The dagger sticking out of the back of her neck is nice, but Axel wants to see her face and the tip of the blade protruding from the front for his picture. He pulls the chair over and sits her down onto it... FLASH. 'That's a good one.'

Axel pulls the chair, with her in it, back across the room to the small desk. He gets out his fingerprint paper that has a space sectioned off for all ten fingers. He grabs her limp right hand and moves her right thumb onto her bloody neck wound. He directs the thumb to the paper marked right thumb and presses down with a rolling motion. He slowly and methodically does this for all ten fingers. Then he carries her to the bathroom sink and washes the blood from her fingertips.

The next thing to address is the DNA he left in her mouth. Axel's not worried that it will lead the cops to him. They don't have a sample from him to compare against. But if he leaves his DNA on more than one victim, they will know there's a serial killer somewhere. For tonight's cover-up, he goes into his bag and pulls out... a blowtorch.

Axel removes the dagger from Maria's neck. It doesn't come out easily. He has to lay her on the ground, face down, and hold his foot against the back of her head to pull the dagger out without lifting her whole body up. He rolls her over again, so she's face up, and lights the torch. He proceeds to completely burn the inside of her mouth and deep down the inside of her throat. He had told her to swallow, but he was in her mouth when he came, and she was in no condition to swallow after that. He's satisfied that all the semen is burned off.

Axel puts Maria back on the bed, washes his fingerprints off the dagger, and leaves it next to her. He takes a quick shower to get all the blood off himself and changes clothes.
Axel always keeps an inventory in his head of anything he touches with a hard surface. He wipes down everywhere his fingerprints could be. He puts on latex gloves and opens Maria's purse... damn, no cash! This hobby usually makes Axel a few bucks, but tonight has been a financially bust. Axel carefully packs up his things and it's time to head home.

He stops at a bonfire pit on the beach before leaving Tijuana. It's the middle of the night, so nobody's around. He casually starts a fire and dumps his bloody clothes and used latex gloves in it. Confident that he destroyed all links back to himself or any evidence of a serial killer, he drives across the border and back home. No reason for anyone to believe this was anything but an isolated incident. Any investigation will only lead to people she knows. I would guess the most likely suspect is Pedro, her fat pimp… probably sending a violent message to his other girls not to take side jobs without cutting him in.

When he arrives home, Axel is exhausted. But he's compelled to take care of his filing. He staples the two pictures of Maria to the page with her red fingerprints. He spaces them out so that neither are obstructed by the other on the page. He lifts up a floorboard in his bedroom and removes a thick binder. He opens the binder and adds Maria to the back. He flips through the binder. There must be well over 100 pages in there! Axel stops at the first page and remembers his first … Vicky.

Before Vicky, Axel was a fairly normal person… or at least not so abnormal. He was not physically or sexually abused as a child. He had a relatively normal family. He was able to interact with his environment like any other human: did well in school, had a few friends and girlfriends, didn't drink or do drugs too often, didn't overuse pornography.

Maybe most serial killers are normal, intelligent people, like Axel. (That is, normal except for the desire to kill people). The typical serial killer profile is based on the ones that got caught.

But those psychopaths wanted to get caught, even if only sub-consciously.

Most murders are never solved. What if those murders can be attributed to serial killers who don't fit the serial killer profile? These guys (or gals) don't get caught, so they don't get analyzed and profiled. If they've evolved enough to be intentionally random, they have a decisive advantage over anyone trying to stop them. It's human nature to hide what you don't want others to see. Is it hard to believe there are people out there who kill and effectively cover it up just because others kill and leave patterns?

Back to Axel's binder: Vicky is his only victim that Axel doesn't have Polaroids or fingerprints of. She was *almost* and accident. In his binder, for her page, is a driver's license and a newspaper article which has a small black and white photo of her. It's dated about ten years ago and is from Atlantic City, New Jersey. It's not an article about a murder; it is a missing persons story...

Ten years ago: Axel was having a bad day. He had been seeing a girl a couple weeks. He lived in Philadelphia and she lived in Atlantic City, about an hour away. He drove over to pay her a surprise visit. When she answered the door, Axel could see past the doorway to the kitchen table (set for two) and a guy seated and drinking a glass of wine. This pissed Axel off, but he was not so invested in the relationship to stick around, so he just took off. She tried to half-ass explain as Axel walked away, but nothing registered in Axel's mind. He was seeing red and it was just background noise.

Axel drove off. He needed a drink and stopped at a casino bar.

Axel was upset and had lots of pent up aggression. After he downed a couple shots of whiskey alone at a back table, Vicky approached him; he didn't know she was a prostitute.

Vicky was absolutely stunning, much hotter than the tramp he drove all this way for. She was a redhead. Axel usually wasn't partial to redheads; he preferred brunettes, and blondes were next, but it was a dark shade of red that worked on her. Her complexion was light-skinned, like most redheads, but not freckled at all. She filled out a tight black dress with a supermodel's body: long legs, thin waste, and what looked like full D-cup size breasts. Axel's a decent looking guy, but she's way out of his league.

They talked for at least an hour. In this short period of time, Axel felt some type of connection with her. Both were buzzed and the conversation quickly became about sex (she steered it that way to gain a customer, but Axel didn't get it). Vicky confided things she liked, and she liked it rough: spanking, hair pulling, choking. She invited him back to her motel room a short walk away. Once there, she made it more clear that she was a prostitute. Axel and his ego were devastated, but he was past the point of no return, so he agreed to pay her.

The sex was passionate …and rough. Axel was on top of her and she was facing him. This was Axel's first time with a prostitute, but it was much more intimate than he previously conceived it could be with somebody he was paying for sex. He frequented many prostitutes after this, but none ever rivaled this experience.

Vicky was building up to an orgasm and demanded, "I'm gonna cum. Grab my throat!" She moved his hand to her neck. This excited Axel and he squeezed. Vicky was having the strongest orgasm Axel ever witnessed.

But she'd been cumming for what felt like a full minute. The combination of her orgasming and his squeezing her throat turned Axel on so much, he was going to cum too…

He remembers vividly her pulling at his hand and her face turning red. But Axel kept squeezing harder and harder… he needed just a few more seconds. He was completely lost in the moment. And it kept building and building until she was no longer struggling, and he exploded inside her. He didn't let up on her throat until another minute went by, just laying there on top of her.

No doubt at all that she was dead.

Axel had to think fast. He didn't mean to do it. He didn't know what to do, but he knew he was in trouble if he didn't figure it out. Still, he didn't panic. First and foremost, he had used a condom, so he carefully flushed it down the toilet and flushed it two more times to make sure it was gone. His saliva was on

Vicky, and possibly a stray pubic hair, so he put her in the tub and washed her. He looked around the room and thought about what else could possibly lead someone to him. There would be his fingerprints, but it was a motel room, there would be lots of fingerprints around from any period of time. But he looked around the room for anything he might have touched and wiped it all clean with bath towels.

Axel thinks… how do I get rid of the body? Then he realizes… nobody knows I was here. He didn't have anything to do with checking into the motel, so maybe he could just leave Vicky here and walk back to his car in the casino parking lot. Could it really be that easy?

Out of curiosity, Axel wraps his fingers with toilet paper and goes through Vicky's purse. He finds a little over $2500.00. He wonders how many other guys she had worked for today. Axel takes the money - she's not gonna need it. He finds her driver's license: Miriam Jones… with black hair - technically, still not partial to redheads then. He thinks to himself, 'I thought those jet black pubes on a redhead didn't look quite right.' Axel takes the drivers license, but he's not sure why. (There are other items left in her purse that identify her by name).

Axel watches the news and checks the newspaper every day, but there's never a report about her. He goes to a payphone and calls the police station to check on Miriam Jones, but there's never any information available. After a month goes by, he catches a small newspaper story that describes Miriam Jones as a missing person. How could nobody discover the body after a month? A maid would have had to check that room within a day or two, right?

Axel is never sure what eventually happened to Vicky's body (he prefers to think of her as Vicky). His best guess is that she was affiliated with the mob - it WAS Atlantic City, and she WAS a hooker. If they set her up in that room and later found her there, they sure as hell wouldn't want the cops involved. They could have dropped her in the ocean and nobody ever found her. That was Axel's best guess at least.

Chapter 2

The Need Escalates

Axel puts the binder back under the floorboard and goes to sleep.

The next several days are uneventful. Axel goes to work at the locksmith shop; he does his job well. He's been there two years and is well liked and by co-workers and customers. Axel is friendly, but for the most part could be described as quiet, a loner. When your whole life's a secret, there is not much to talk about. Most importantly, Axel doesn't have a creepy vibe about him that would scare people off; he genuinely seems trustworthy. He is a decent looking guy, 37 years old, tall, keeps fit, but he's not overly good looking. He blends in.

As far as anyone here knows, he lived in Philadelphia all his life and moved to LA two years ago when he started working at the locksmith shop. But Axel has been a rolling stone, moving every few months to a year for the past 10 years. Can't get too comfortable in one place when murders have to be spread out geographically. But he's stayed in LA for two years by making road trips and being cleverly random.

That dizzy feeling that happened in Mexico has happens a few more times. It's accompanied by a whispering type of sound resembling a woman's tone, but Axel can't make out anything as being words that she's saying. These episodes only last a few seconds at a time.

Axel normally spaces out his hunts to no more than once a month or so, but it's been a week since Mexico, and he is having strong cravings. He decides to browse the internet. There are several sites he knows of where call girls essentially post classified ads with pictures: the internet age, shopping for call girls has never been more convenient. He contacts Jessica by instant message and arranges to call her. The deal is struck: $500.00 for the evening's festivities. Axel tells her to pick a hotel and check in the room. He'll meet her there and pay her back for the room. Axel claims that he's married and can't have a hotel room show up on his credit card bill. The second half of that statement is very true. She has no problem with this and says to meet her at the hotel at 8:00pm.

Axel has lots of time before he has to leave. He prepares his travel bag. First he puts on latex gloves to not get fingerprints on anything he's packing. He's never touched his fingerprint paper without gloves on, and every weapon he has is wiped clean if they ever touch his bare fingers. Axel is meticulous.

He adds to the bag: fingerprint paper, Polaroid camera, four different sized knives, a surgical scalpel, duct tape, four pairs of handcuffs, three different kinds of rope, blindfold, four pairs of latex gloves, blowtorch, needle nose pliers, two large plastic garbage bags, acid (the type to burn through flesh), two shirts, two pairs of jeans, one pair of shoes, rags, and a disposable phone with prepaid minutes, not registered or traceable (Axel keeps several of these phones and throws them out if necessary).

He also keeps a large trunk and a large duffle bag in the trunk of his car in case a plan goes awry and he has to move a body. Everything has a purpose, but only a few items get used in an evening.

When it is time to leave, Axel is calm yet excited. This is what he lives for. But as he is approaching his car with his bag, he gets another one of his dizzy spells that brings him to the ground this time. He hears the distorted female voice… it kinda sounds like she's laughing.

Axel looks around, composes himself, and gets in his car. He pulls onto the road and gets a call from Jessica. She's arrived and is in room 204. He drives a few blocks past the hotel and looks for a place to park on the street. He doesn't want his car seen too close to the crime scene, and he's careful to not park anywhere that might be videotaping for security. He takes the stairs, not the elevator; he wears a baseball cap and mostly faces his head downward so any camera in the ceiling should not get a good look at his face.

Axel knocks. Jessica answers the door … She is NOT quite what her pictures look like on the web. She's about 10 - 20 pounds heavier and looks about 10 years older. Market rate for this bitch should be about $200.00 at best. But Axel's not really paying anyway, so what the hell. And he can carve off the extra weight if it really bothers him. She looks like a tweeker … how do you get an overweight tweeker? …And one that knows how to use Photoshop so well?

She greets him with, "Hi Hugh, come on in … do you have the money, the room was $120.00." By the way Axel uses the alias Hugh Johnson for these encounters. It's clever, no?

Axel sets his bag down inside and peels off $620.00 for Jessica. She's just lit a cigarette and holds it between her lips as she counts the cash. Axel quips, "You shouldn't smoke. Those things'll kill ya."

Immediately Axel is hearing another female voice in the room, but he can't understand anything she's saying or where it's coming from. He questions, "Jessica, you're alone here, right?"

She answers, "Yes, it's just us. You ready to party, baby?" she starts disrobing. Axel starts coming around - she doesn't look all THAT bad; He was expecting a 9 …she's a do-able 6 ½.

He decides to play with his toy before breaking it. He puts on a condom and fucks her in several positions. She has a good work ethic if nothing else. It's been about an hour of non-stop sex and Axel can tell she wants him to cum REALLY bad already. She gets on top and really works it … with her hips and with her (very fake) moaning. They're both gleaming with sweat. Axel enjoys it, but Jessica can't make him cum, not just from sex. But she's going at it, full speed ahead.

Then Axel sees something out of the corner of his eye in the bathroom. He didn't get a good look, but it seemed like the figure of a dark-haired woman.

He pushes Jessica off him and dashes toward the bathroom. "What the fuck?... I thought you said we were alone!" ...But as he checks, nobody is in the bathroom.

Jessica is confused, sitting up naked on the bed, "What are you talking about? Nobody IS here... Stop tripping and finish fucking me."

Axel hears a female voice; it's faint and distorted, but he hears, "What are the handcuffs for?" This freezes him up. He realizes that Jessica isn't seeing or hearing what he is. Then, another dizzy spell that drops Axel to the ground.

Jessica's now getting scared of him, but not scared the way Axel wants; she just thinks he's a wierdo. Jessica stands and starts putting her panties on, she's had enough. Axel, still on his hands and knees from the dizzy spell, offers, "Wait... I'll give you another $1000.00 to stay... and let me handcuff you to the bed."

Now Jessica is frozen for a moment, panties half way up her legs, "Are you ok? Are you even able to screw now?" she says looking at him (and his limp penis) on the ground.

"Yes, you put on the handcuffs and this thing will spring right back up, I promise." He stands up and goes to his bag.

She takes her panties off again and says, "Let's see the money first... And I'm gonna need something from my bag too."

Axel counts off the money and she goes to her bag, for some lube.

Axel pulls out two pairs of the handcuffs and cuffs each of her wrists to the bedpost. She's face up with her arms spread, almost fully extended, to each side of the king size bed. Axel sees that flash of a dark-haired woman in the corner of his eye, but just as he turns, she's gone again.

Axel is unfazed this time and goes back to his bag - this time getting out the duct tape. Jessica looks concerned, "What are you gonna do with that?" Axel coolly replies, "Do you trust me?" and grins. "Well, sure, but you should be fucking me right now not ..." Axel rips a piece of duct tape off and seals her mouth. He looks down, "See, I told you it would spring right back up." He adjusts the condom back in place.

Axel can't see or hear the mysterious dark-haired female, but he can somehow feel her presence. He feels like he has an audience ... and he likes it. It motivates him. But this fact does not fare well for Jessica.

He pulls out the two remaining pairs of handcuffs. Jessica is kicking and muffled pissed-off yells are coming from behind the duct tape. Axel cuffs her right ankle and then attaches the other end to the bedrail, and then her left ankle. She's restrained by all four limbs to the bed, completely helpless.

Axel removes the camera from his bag and 'FLASH', he has a 'living' shot. Next, Axel contemplates his many choices and removes... a paring knife from the selection in his bag. He climbs on top of Jessica, grabs her lube bottle, and applies a handful to her pussy. Then her penetrates her with his dick and rests his bodyweight completely on top of her so that she can't move. He looks Jessica right in the eyes. He can taste her fear, and he can't get enough. He smiles, and she head-butts him, ruining the mood for a moment.

Axel laughs a little, still lying flat on top of her and inside her. He takes the paring knife in his right hand and jabs it all the way into her left outer thigh while keeping eye contact. It's about a 2 ½ inch blade and Jessica screams in pain, but very little sound escapes the duct tape. Then, Axel gives the knife a little twist and jets his cock in and out of her a few times.

That's enough of the romantic stuff. Axel lifts his upper body and holds himself up with his extended left arm, leaving his right arm free. He pulls the knife out of Jessica's thigh, leaving his penis in her, and makes a sideways puncture into her left breast. It goes through the outer side traveling to the center of her tit, but the knife isn't long enough to come through the other side. He removes the knife to gaze at the wound. Now there's blood covering a large portion of that side of the bed.

Axel lays the bloody knife on the center of Jessica's chest and rubs his fingers on her breast wound. He wipes up some blood and smears it on her face and across the duct tape over her mouth. In her eyes is pain and fear and desperation, and tears are flowing. She knows she's going to die.

Axel picks the knife back up from her chest and looks at her inviting arms spread wide apart. He jabs the knife into her left wrist about an inch deep and rips the blade all of the way down her arm to her armpit. This causes a LOT more bleeding. They're both getting soaked in red – it's glorious to Axel. Jessica is now clearly in shock; she's not struggling as much as before. Axel knows this is as good as it's going to get.

With blood everywhere already, he thrusts his cock faster and faster into her, stabbing her in the belly every few seconds; he vowed to himself to save the throat kill for another day. She has about 8 punctures to the midsection now, but none are more than an inch or two deep, so she's not quite dying yet. But Axel feels the need to climax. So he plunges the knife one last time, as deep as the blade will go, into her stomach, and leaves it in her. He pinches her nose tightly and Jessica's eyes get wide. She was already breathing very heavy to stay alive while bleeding out, so it's not more than a few seconds before this snuffs the last trace of life from Jessica's body. She goes completely limp.

Axel mires at the red designs he painted over this hotel room canvas and pulls his cock out of lifeless Jessica.

He flushes the condom … three times.

Axel's after-kill procedures and cleanup have become routine for him after so many years. It's not a chore, but it is careful and methodical. Axel takes his 'after' picture. He then unlocks all of the handcuffs and takes Jessica's bloody fingerprints onto his special paper, one by one. Then he washes the blood off her fingertips. (If the cops see a string of victims with bloody fingertips, that could be a pattern, alerting them of a serial killer). He doesn't have to worry about leaving traces of his pubic hair any more, because years ago, he began shaving completely down there to avoid that problem. Take a thorough shower, put on clean clothes. Wipe fingerprints from everything: from the knife to the lube to the handcuffs. Leave the knife and handcuffs behind but pack up everything else. Anything that touched her blood will be burned when he gets home.

And of course, Axel takes his money back. First put on latex gloves to open her purse. Remove the $1620.00 of his money on top that he gave her. What else do we have here … baggie of white powder, she IS a tweeker. (drops the baggie to the ground). OK, open wallet … credit card, credit card, credit card, library card(???), cash - two dollars, Fuck! I was supposed to make up for my losses in Mexico (pockets the $2.00). Looks at her ID: surprising, her name really was Jessica. Appointment card for her gynecologist … prenatal vitamins … holly shit, Jessica must have been pregnant! That explains the extra weight. A 2'fer killing … Probably did the world a favor tonight. With a tweeker prostitute for a mom, that kid would have had the typical upbringing to be…a serial killer!

All packed up, baseball hat back on, time to go. Before carefully opening the door to leave, Axel takes one last look back towards Jessica, and on the wall, above the bed, he sees 'THANK YOU' written in blood. In an instant, it fades away and completely disappears. He stops for a moment, confused. As he opens the door, he hears a female whisper say, "I'm... getting... stronger."

Axel begins to question his own senses... But it all seemed so real.

Axel knows the smart thing to do is take some time off from killing for a while until he can get his head together. The next few days are pretty routine. Work is normal. But he still gets the dizzy spells, and now they sometimes come with a sharp pain in his head. But they still only last a few seconds and then they're completely gone.

Saturday comes a few days later, and these urges that Axel used to keep in check, for months at a time if necessary, are too strong to resist. He packs his bag and drives into Hollywood... the Sunset Strip.

He spots a corner with two working girls and pulls up for a closer look. Both come over to his passenger window to chat. One is an attractive black girl and she's closer to the window. She reaches in to rub on his shoulder. Axel has killed a few black girls before in other states, but he hasn't killed one in LA yet. He considers her for a moment, especially to add to his randomness, but he doesn't get a good vibe from her.

The other hooker, upon closer examination... looks kinda manly? Axel looks in her direction and floats, "What's up?" She replies in a deep, husky, throaty voice, "Hi Sugar, I'm Amanda. Wanna take a walk on the wild side?"

Definitely a transsexual! Great name – Amanda… She's A Man… Duh.

Though this definitely would add to his randomness, Axel decides to pass and move on.

A few blocks down, he sees a bleached blonde who's smoking a cigarette. She's wearing the tightest, trashiest, most revealing dress he's seen yet tonight with giant (fake) boobs just about falling out. She has the full hooker make-up on and cliché ridiculously high heels, but she has a raw trashy appeal. Axel pulls up next to where she's standing and makes eye contact. But before he can speak, a BIG guy Axel didn't see, who was behind her in the shadow, steps forward, "What the fuck are you looking at?!!!" And he puts his arm around her and steers her away from the street… Must not have been a hooker?

Axel does a U-turn to try the other side of the street. A little further up, he sees a woman on the sidewalk in front of a motel parking lot. She looks much classier than the blonde from a moment ago, but he's still sure she's waiting for a trick to come along. As he gets closer, he knows she's the one he wants. There's something about her; it's an instant attraction. She resembles Vicky from Atlantic City, just a little. No doubt it wasn't Vicky, but they could've been sisters. She has red hair, redder than Vicky's hair was, a similar complexion, and similar facial features. Vicky was prettier in his memory, but he's fascinated by this new one.

He pulls up and decides to lay more down on the table. "Hi darling." She walks over to his passenger window, "Looking for some company?"

Axel says, "I'm looking for more than company. Why don't you get in and talk to me?"

She says, "I'm Trixie. Turn off the engine so we can talk." Axel turns off the engine and she opens the car door, sits down, but leaves the door all of the way open (for her safety presumably).

Trixie: "What did you have in mind? I'm an open-minded kinda girl."

Axel: "I like that. I have a large budget for this evening, but I need to know you're willing to do what I need."

Trixie: "I think I'm up for it. TRY to surprise me" (in a challenging tone)

Axel: "I'll start the bidding at $2000.00 if you're prepared to be tied up, smacked around… and your ass isn't off limits."

Trixie: "Let me see the cash."

Axel opens his wallet…

Just then, three male cops come rushing over to the car. BUSTED! She's a cop, and Axel got stung. She's wearing a wire. They cuff Axel, read him his rights, and sit him on the curb. Trixie pulls her cop car from behind the motel over to the scene. She locks Axel in the back seat.

Now that things are under control, two of the male cops walk behind the motel, get in their car, and drive away. Officer Megan White (aka Trixie) and Officer Craig Carter perform a routine search on Axel's car. They find his bag in the trunk. Axel is sitting, watching this from the back of the cop car. He can see and hear everything they're doing. He sits calmly, but is naturally concerned about what will happen to him once they see the knives and ropes and handcuffs and blowtorch and pliers and latex gloves... There's nothing he can think of to explain why he has these things in his trunk.

He rationalizes that there's nothing there that directly links him to a crime. His planning was meticulous, no need to panic now. It looks incriminating as hell. They could say that he was about to do something awful. But American justice doesn't work like that: best to be quiet and ride it out.

Axel watches as Craig opens the bag. He can hear everything they're saying. Megan is taking notes in her notepad. Craig verbalizes to Megan as he removes items from the bag. Craig lifts out… "fingerprint paper…" "surgical scalpel…" "1, 2, 3 …4 pairs of handcuffs …" "large hunting knife…" Craig pauses and displays the knife to Megan, "This is a fuckin' serious knife."

It's an expensive fancy piece from a cutlery shop. It looks like something out of the medieval age: very long blade with crescent cutouts to create extra points along the edge and a con-

33

toured handle with cutouts to fit each finger. It's very sharp and has an intimidating look.

Megan stops him, "Craig, this is serious. This isn't just a John. This guy could've killed somebody. We need to bag this stuff."

Craig agrees with Megan, so he gets clear evidence bags out of his trunk and puts on his own latex gloves. They proceed to log in all of the items in Axel's bag.

As this goes on, both cops continually glare over at Axel in judgment over what they're finding. Craig gets into the drivers seat of the car and Megan gets in the front passenger seat. Craig calls dispatch for a tow of Axel's car. He tells them not to take it to the usual impound lot: take it to forensics for a thorough inspection. The bag of weapons gives them probable cause to do this. They begin to work on Axel as they drive to the police station:

Craig: "Why do you have those weapons in your car Axel? What did you have planned for Trixie here?"

Axel says nothing.

Craig: "We already have you taped, and you're gonna spend the night in jail as a John. We're gonna go through every inch of your vehicle and they're going to examine every item in your bag. If there's ANYTHING there, the slightest trace of blood, anything at all, we got you."

Megan: "Don't you have anything to say for yourself? Is there any reasonable explanation you care to offer."

34

Axel stays silent.

They get to the police station, and Axel is booked. He considers the fingerprinting to be slightly ironic and can't help but smile a little while they do it; they are using the exact same paper Axel uses. This is the first time he's been arrested for anything, so this is his first time being fingerprinted.

He can only be charged with patronizing a prostitute, so that is the pretext to keep him in jail for now. If not for the suspicious bag, he would've paid a fine and already be home. But the cops know the clock is ticking, because this charge is only a misdemeanor. They have three days and then they have to let him go.

Over the next three days the police search Axel's car and find nothing. Police forensics thoroughly examine the items in Axel's bag and find no blood or anything that implicates him to a crime. They interrogate him for hours at a time, but they can't break him. Still, Axel's smug demeanor only reinforces Craig and Megan's intuition that he's guilty of something heinous.

They have to let Axel go in just a few hours. Craig and Megan go to their captain and look for new angles they can investigate Axel. They really want to search Axel's house, but the captain tells them that no judge will give a search warrant based on what they have. They don't have an actual crime or victim, just the tools to commit a crime. If there isn't evidence that he's already DONE something, he can't be held.

Megan is upset and frustrated, but Craig is taking this very personally. He knows in his gut that Axel either has murdered someone or is going to, and POSSIBLY, more than one person. Craig is disgusted that he can't do anything about it. The system sucks!

Axel is released. Axel is given all of his personal items back. Axel is given his car back.

He puts the items, each one still in the police's clear plastic baggies, back into his original bag, places it all in his trunk, and drives away. Craig is boiling as he watches Axel drive off, still fixated on getting him.

Chapter 3

What Happens In Vegas...

The next day Axel goes into the locksmith shop. He's missed three days of work without calling in. He explains that his grandfather in Philadelphia passed away and he had to go for the funeral. Sorry, he forgot to call in... No repercussions there.

As he's working, he notices Craig and Megan looking in the shop from the street. When Axel goes out on a call to replace locks in a house, Craig and Megan follow and park by the house to watch him for a while. When he goes home, they're waiting in their car in front of his house. This continues for a couple days. The message is very clear: they were watching him. Axel even notices Craig watching him, out of uniform, on what must be his off hours. And random other patrol cars seem to be slowing around his house and his work fairly often. It might be time to relocate to another state.

The next weekend comes, and Axel knows he has to get away, even if just for a couple days for now... Las Vegas.

Vegas is about a four hour drive across empty desert, far enough away that there won't be any cops hassling him there. He packs clothes and a new bag of killing supplies, leaving the old bag in his closet. For some reason, he doesn't want to use those, like they were somehow tainted by the cops. But he doesn't want to throw them out either - just an instinct.

Before he drives into the city of Las Vegas he stops for gas (pays cash of course). He finds a car with Nevada plates that is parked out of anyone's immediate vision. He casually kneels down and unscrews the license plates and takes them. Once back on the highway, he drives a few miles, pulls over and replaces his plates with the new ones and puts his plates in his trunk. Just a precaution, lots of cameras in Vegas, and Axel doesn't want anyone to know he was ever there.

Axel has no interest in gambling. He finds the smallest, seediest motel on the outskirts of town, far from the strip. He partly disguises himself with a fake beard and mustache, a long blonde wig and a cowboy hat, and he uses a fake Texan accent. It's just enough misdirection that a guy at the desk, who sees lots of people in a day, shouldn't remember his face if he sees him again. He checks in with a cash bribe under his alias, Hugh Johnson.

Axel's been using hookers for his last few victims, but it almost feels like cheating to him - it's so easy. He usually seeks out more creative ways to target victims, and Vegas is full of opportunities. Women are much more likely to have a one night stand when they're far from home. There's a bar about a quarter mile from his motel. Axel decides to walk over and see if he can pick someone up and get her voluntarily back to his room.

Axel enters the bar, and immediately there are several women that pique his interest. But Axel soon notices that there are slot machines in the bar. He looks up to the ceiling; there are cameras everywhere. He can't kill someone he's been recorded talking to and leaving with.

He leaves the bar, looking for a more discrete opportunity. As he walks down the sidewalk, there's a newspaper dispenser machine that catches his eye. He opens it and takes a copy... In the family friendly city of Las Vegas, these newspaper stands contain free magazines that are nothing but sex ads - lots of call girls to choose from, very convenient and discreet.

Axel feels an instant liking for one of the girls advertised... She's calling to him, so he decides to take the easy route once again. She's an S & M girl named Mistress Kendra. She's dressed in black leather and is holding a whip. Her ad says, 'I've been a bad girl... I can dish it out... or I can take it'. Axel knows she'll be 'taking it' this time. It also says, 'Nobody beats my beatings.'

Axel calls and asks if the picture in the paper is a good representation of her (he didn't want a repeat of the last chick from the internet). She confirms it's a recent picture; she's tall with brown hair, an athletic body, and medium sized tits. She says she's 32 (which corresponds with the picture). She asks if he wants her to dominate him, or if he wants to dominate her. Axel confirms that he wants her to be the submissive. Her price is $1000.00 – 1500.00 without sex, depending how extreme the session is, and $2000.00 for the whole package with sex. The price is agreed at $2000.00, and she'll bring plenty of extras to play with.

Axel prepares for Mistress Kendra's arrival. He closes the drapes tightly and opens his bag to consider his choices. He hasn't slit a throat in a while. He deserves a treat after all he's been through, and he IS far from home.

He hears that now familiar female voice, "Use the big knife." He looks around the small motel room and bathroom. He checks under the bed. He opens the door to look around outside. As he expected, nobody's there. He goes back inside and closes the door.

He hears, "I've been watching you." For the first time, Axel acknowledges the voice and talks back into the air, "Who is that? …What do you want?" He hears her whisper, "Axel" from directly behind him. He turns and sees her for an instant and then her image fades away. But he saw her … it was a dark-haired woman. Could it be a ghost? "Are you a ghost?" …No answer.

Then, Axel sees the large hunting knife levitate from his bag and tuck itself between the mattress and boxspring of the bed. He lifts the mattress to see if it's really there... It is not! He checks his bag and the knife is right where he left it... Still, that knife isn't a bad choice.

There's a knock at the door; Mistress Kendra has arrived. Axel opens the door. She's in a long black trench coat and has a large bag of her own. Kendra enters and drops her trench coat to the ground. Underneath is definitely a mistress's uniform: long black boots that go halfway up her thigh with thin 5 inch heels, short black leather mini-skirt with metal trimmings, a leather bustier with holes that her nipples are poking through, a black leather collar with metal rings designed to attach to a leash or some other type of restraint, wristbands with metal studs and the same type of metal rings. She has many piercings already visible: lip, nose, navel, and both nipples. This chick's not fooling around.

Her first words after dropping the coat and giving Axel a moment to take it all in: "Money please."

Axel gives her $2000.00. As she counts it, she sets some ground rules. "I brought some restraints, some whips, a paddle, and a pony kit. That last thing is a butt plug with a pony tail on the end, so once inserted in my ass, or your ass, whatever turns you on, will look like a pony's tail. We can do whatever you want, but the $2000 only covers the next hour and a half. If you want to talk first, the meter's still running. This is important: If I say the word 'DRAGON', you have to stop what you are doing immediately. Dragon is my safe word. You can be plenty rough, but don't push beyond my limits."

Axel promises to obey the 'dragon' command and acts naïve, as if he's never done anything like this before. He looks through her stuff. He IS impressed. She has a cool set of restraints he decides to try out.

Each restraint is essentially a sturdy metal rod about 3 feet long with leather cuffs at each end. While Mistress Kendra stands, Axel fastens both cuffs to Kendra's wrists which force her hands to remain 3 feet apart from each other, separated by

41

the rod. He didn't think about taking her top off before attaching these restraints, so it will be staying on now. But before restraining her legs, he unzips her mini-skirt and pulls it to the ground; and then he pulls her sheer black panties slowly to the ground... Hey look…another piercing!

He takes her other restraint of the same type out of her bag, leads her to sit on the bed, and attaches it to her ankles, over her boots. He knows he will have to restrain her further later on, but this is good enough while she's still a willing participant. Her hands have been to her sides with the restraint bar on her lap. Once her ankles are locked in place, she lifts her hands above her head and slides back in the bed, face up. It is an extremely sexy visual: Bottomless, spread eagle with that leather top on that has her nipples poking through, super high boots and rods holding her arms and legs apart.

Axel asks if he can take her picture. She vehemently refuses, "Absolutely not!"

"OK," Axel knows he will get his picture eventually. "I'm gonna have to punish you then."

He pulls a bullwhip out of Kendra's bag and takes a crack on her stomach. She gives a little wince and it leaves a red mark. But she seems to be a good sport so far. He swings the whip two more times, harder than before. She gives him a lustful look. He thinks, 'Holly shit, this is my type of girl.'

Axel pulls out a fringy lighter type of whip called a cat of 9 tales. He takes a few slashes in between her spread legs at her pussy. The first couple swipes land slightly to the right and slightly to the left, but the next couple land right on target and she flinches, but no sign of the word dragon.

Like a kid in a sadistic candy store Axel takes out her paddle from her bag. It's a pretty thick, heavy piece of wood with a heart shape cut through. He rolls Kendra over and takes a hard swing at her ass with the paddle. She lets out a quiet "ah" in pain. But she seems to like it. There's a bright red mark about 5 inches wide (the width of the paddle) across her ass, with a white heart left in her flesh corresponding to the cutout in the wood. In Axel's mind: 'Cool. I'm keeping this thing... Anyone can beat a chick with a 2 x 4, but the heart shape shows you care.'

He smacks her with the paddle a few more times, very hard. Her ass is getting bright red, and there's no trace of any white hearts any more. Still no 'dragon'. He goes back to the heavier bull whip and cracks it across her reddened ass as hard as he could. That gets a loud, "Ahh, fuck, dragon... dragon!"

Axel stops as promised and acts concerned' "Are you ok?"

"Yes, just no more on my ass today. Are you still wanting to fuck, or do you just want to beat me?"

Axel replies, "I'm ready to fuck... This was some GREAT foreplay, so thank you for that... I'm shy. I want you to stay face down and close your eyes while I get undressed."

Axel doesn't want her to scream as he goes in his bag for his duct tape. He walks back to her, rips off a piece, and covers her mouth before she knows what's happening.

Axel explains, "OK, say 'dragon' if I go too far," and he punches her in the face. Although her wrists are fixed 3 feet apart, she may be able to stretch her head to one of her hands to remove the tape and Axel knows to prevent this. Also, she can still move around the room, bounce off walls, or break the window if he's not careful. So he grabs the rod that holds her wrists and drags her over to his bag across the room. He takes out some rope, drags her back to the bed, and ties the metal rods to the top and bottom of the bed. She's face down and properly restrained.

Axel gets the camera from his bag, kneels by the bed and lifts her left wrist upward so that her face and body turn up, toward him. "OK if I take your picture now?" 'FLASH.' Got his 'before' picture.

Axel picks up the large hunting knife and is considering his many options for a moment when, out of the corner of his eye, he sees that vision of the black-haired woman in the room again. Axel turns toward her. She's smiling; she's clearly not disgusted by what she's seeing. He approaches her, grabs her by the throat and presses her back against the wall. He can feel her, so she must be real, "Who are you? How the fuck did you get in here?"

Axel holds the knife to her throat. He notices bruising all around her neck. She's not scared at all; she giggles a little. This angers Axel more. "Wait, I remember you... Vicky??? ...Your hair was different... I killed you 10 years ago."

She just chuckles some more, and almost as a reflex out of fear and confusion and anger, Axel cuts her throat. She falls to the ground producing a large puddle of blood on the floor beneath her... apparently dead? Axel backs away from her and looks back over towards the bed to glance at Kendra: still struggling but fully restrained. He turns back to look at Vicky on the floor, but when he looks back, Vicky is gone somehow. But he sees the puddle of blood she left still there, and it slowly fades and vanishes in front of his eyes. He touches the carpet and it is completely dry. He doesn't know what just happened, but his adrenaline is pumping.

Axel focusses his attention back to Kendra. First he wants a little more foreplay. He picks the paddle back up and whacks her ass several times. He can't see her face, but he can hear her muffled screams and can tell she's crying. This must be painful! He takes his large hunting knife and cuts her top off to expose some virgin pale skin on her back. He bull whips her back at least 20 times ...he loses count.

All this foreplay has Axel fully aroused. He undresses, puts on a condom and fucks Kendra from behind as she lays restrained flat on her stomach. Axel is so turned on it only takes a couple minutes until he's ready. He grabs a handful of her hair and pulls it back toward him. This lifts her chin up and back, exposing the front of her throat. She's fully alert and alarmed, and crying and trying to scream. Axel slowly moves this large, intimidating hunting knife in front of her face so she can gaze upon it and know what's coming. She panics and struggles more, but she can't move much.

Axel hears the mystery woman's voice again like a whisper into his right ear, "Please... stop teasing... Cut her throat." Axel checks to the right; nothing's there, so he dismisses it, like it never happened.

Axel, completely focused on Kendra, moves the knife to her throat and slices deep with a fast hard motion. Blood pours out of her neck, onto the wall and pillows, and down her neck and chest. She makes a gurgling sound and her body goes limp. Axel's just climaxed and is listening for any subtle sounds that may come from Kendra as she passes.

But the sound he hears is coming from behind him - quiet sexy moaning? He turns to look. It's Vicky, standing at the foot of the bed. She's facing him, mostly undressed, with nothing but a white unbuttoned blouse and a pair of white silky panties. Her left hand is inside her blouse on her right breast, and her right hand is in her underwear with her fingers circling. Her moans get a little louder.

Axel can't believe what he's seeing, but he just watches as she climaxes. Vicky then looks over Kendra's beaten bloody dead body, makes eye contact with Axel, gives him a wicked grin, and slowly fades away.

Once again, for lack of any idea how to react to Vicky's appearance or disappearance, Axel tends to his clean-up. Flush the condom three times, take the after picture, fingerprint Kendra with her own blood and clean her fingers (this time just with wet tissues so he doesn't have to take the time to get her unrestrained and to the sink), shower, get dressed, wipe down anywhere his fingerprints could be (extra diligent now that he's in the system somewhere). Axel puts on his latex gloves and goes to her purse, retrieves his cash and finds an additional $856.00 - A profitable trip. Most people don't leave Vegas with more money than they arrived with. He packs up his things and takes Kendra's paddle.

It's a four hour drive home, which gives Axel time to think. Normally he'd be savoring the memories of his kill, but this time, he can't get Vicky off of his mind. About an hour into the drive, Vicky materializes in the back seat of Axel's car. She startles Axel by putting her hands over his eyes. Axel drifts left into oncoming traffic, but he gets free of Vicky quickly and swerves back into his own lane moments before collision with an oncoming car... Vicky jumps into the front passenger seat.

There's an awkward silence for about 30 long seconds as Axel looks forward at the road. He glances quickly over at Vicky a couple times and then right back to staring at the road ahead. Vicky is staring directly at Axel's face this whole time, patiently waiting for a reaction. She's in a playful mood and knows that her silence is making Axel uncomfortable; he'll have to acknowledge her soon as the tension builds.

Vicky is gorgeous, just as Axel remembered. Except now she has black hair, like her drivers license, instead of red hair. Axel finally does break the silence:

Axel: "You can't be real."

Vicky: "If I wasn't real, could I do this…"

She grabs the top of the steering wheel and pulls it towards her. The car swerves onto the shoulder. Axel corrects and gets back into his lane.

Axel: "OK, stop it! You're real."

There's another 20 second silence.

Axel: "Alright if I call you Vicky? I know your real name is Miriam."

Vicky: "I introduced myself as Vicky, so that would be just fine."

Axel looks over at Vicky and again notices her neck is badly bruised.

Axel: "Sorry about those bruises on your neck… … And about killing you and all, back in Atlantic City… …Oh, and also for cutting your throat earlier tonight."

Vicky: "Your not sorry, you liar." (she says playfully)

Axel: "Ok… please just explain some things to me… What's going on?"

Vicky: "What ever do you mean Axel?" she says coyly.

Axel: "Well if I killed you ten years ago, how the fuck are you here? Are you a ghost?"

Vicky just shrugs, withholding a real answer.

Axel: "Why wait ten years? Why appear and disappear for the last couple weeks?"

Vicky: "Did you ever think that maybe you're appearing and disappearing in my reality? … Just kidding. I don't exactly know your answers. I just am. …I AM here now… But I've been watching you for a long time."

Axel: "Are you my conscience, like the little angel on my shoulder?"

Vicky: (laughs) "Please … you have no conscience, and I'm closer to a little devil on your shoulder."

Axel's mind is moving in many directions at once. He can't get over how sexy she is.

Axel: "I saw you can't be killed earlier, or at least you won't stay dead, right? Can you be fucked?"

Vicky: "Axel, if I can't be killed, do you really even want to fuck me? Think about it."

Axel thinks about it.

Axel: "I must be going crazy, I don't see any other possibility. I don't believe in ghosts and that other crap."

Vicky turns on the radio. Billy Joel is singing, "You may be right … I may be crazy … but it just may be a lunatic you're looking for…"

Axel abruptly turns the station. Ozzy Ozbourne is singing, "I'm going off the rails on a crazy train…"

Vicky turns the station. Quiet Riot is on, "Ma, Mama, we're all crazy now... Ma ma ma ma mama we're all crazy now…"

Axel turns the radio off and there's silence for a few seconds as he absorbs some of this.

Axel: "So at least tell me, what do you want? Are you here for revenge? I know I deserve it... ...Do you have some purpose? ...Do you need my help, like to make something right?"

Vicky: "I'm just winging it and looking for some fun... I think we're gonna have some fun together Axel. We're a team now, and the world is out plague-ground."

Vicky scoots over and rests her head on Axel's shoulder.

After driving a little longer, Vicky notices a sign by the side of the road. She has an idea, but doesn't share it with Axel, not yet.

Later, Vicky asks Axel what he's going to do about the cops that keep hassling him in LA. Axel says he'll probably have to move to another part of the county. He explains:

"I got a good two year run out of the LA area; it's too bad I have to leave. It's a great place to be a serial killer. With the budget deficit of the city, there're never enough police. And the police they have are busy bleeding the population for more cash with traffic citations. Add to that the enormous amount gang violence on a day to day basis, and the result is that each crime doesn't get the kind of attention it would other places. A few months back, our locksmith shop was robbed at gunpoint. They didn't get much, a couple hundred bucks in cash, but when we called 9-1-1, it was over five minutes before they even answered the phone. I could get into just about any house and completely re-strain a woman with five full minutes... And then once we had someone on the phone, it took over an hour for a cop to show up at the shop … for an armed robbery! They took a report, but I don't think they even looked for the robbers at all."

Chapter 4

The Set-Up

A week passes. Axel goes to work and gets visits from Vicky throughout his days. He also gets the dizzy spells and sharp pains in his head several times a day now. Officer Craig and Officer Megan are checking up on him often still. Axel spots them together in uniform, but Craig makes appearances wearing street clothes on his own a lot; he's very persistent. Axel is smart enough to lay low and not kill again in LA, but Vicky is pressuring him to find another victim. She has a stronger blood lust that Axel!

It's been two weeks since Vegas and Vicky convinces Axel to pack a special bag and take a drive. She's excited to be included in picking a victim. They leave Axel's place; no sign of Officer Craig. Good! They head back to the Sunset Strip; after all, Axel didn't get a victim that night - Trixie was a cop.

They spot Amanda working again. Vicky starts to motion to her, but before she can speak, Axel cuts her off, "Absolutely Not!"

Axel's first order of business: drive by the motel to see if there's a sting going on... Yep, there's Trixie (Officer Megan). Drive around back… there's the cop cars... OK, on to business elsewhere. Axel drives down the street.

What Axel and Vicky didn't notice was that Officer Craig was in his personal car by the motel, looking after his partner on his off hours. When he sees Axel, Craig follows him.

Vicky spots a blonde busty hooker. Turns out, Vicky's partial to blondes. Vicky insists that she's their target. Axel parks the car about a block up from the blonde prostitute. He's learned from his last trip to the Sunset Strip... He walks completely around the block on both sides of the street looking for any cops she may be working with. She appears to be a legitimate hooker… how refreshing. Axel approaches her on foot.

Officer Craig has observed Axel from a distance this whole time. But there's a twist… Craig knows this prostitute; he knows her well. Her name is Brooke. Craig knows that she keeps an apartment a few blocks away that she uses for tricks. He goes to that apartment, parks, and waits on her doorstep.

It's not long before Axel and Brooke pull up and walk towards her door. What a surprise for BOTH of them to see this familiar character sitting there in street clothes. Officer Craig begins, "Listen, Brooke, I know what you're thinking, but you don't know about this guy, he's a killer, and if you go in there with him, you…"

Brook cuts him off mid-sentence, "Craig, you mother-fucker! You shouldn't be here! I have a restraining order against you! You're to stay 100 yards away! …I don't believe a word you say, you dirty cop, fucker!… Stop trying to scare away my friend. Just fuckin' leave … now!"

Craig's not at all surprised by her reaction and says, "OK… OK, I tried to warn you… …As for you Axel, I know you're here, I KNOW you'll be on your best behavior tonight."

Craig walks to his car and drives away (9:30pm). He goes home to watch tv, alone. He rationalizes that Brooke is probably safe. Axel didn't seem so stupid as to murder a woman when a cop knows he's there..

Brooke's apartment is just a place she takes her 'clients.' She lives elsewhere, so it doesn't look completely lived in. It's a one bedroom apartment with a small living room, small bathroom and tiny kitchen. The place is mostly empty, except for a bed in the bedroom. But the kitchen is full of stuff to cook with and eat off of, and there are plenty of hard liquor bottles across a shelf. Once inside and in the small living room, Brooke offers a confused looking Axel a drink and an explanation:

"That piece of shit cop busted me for prostitution about six months ago. Instead of arresting me, he said I could give him a freebee and he'd let me go. So I brought him here and did it... The problem was, he thought it was a lifetime pass or something. He'd show up every couple days wanting a freebee. After the third time of him bullying me, I got one of those pens that records audio and kept it on me. The next time he showed up, I recorded everything... I still had to fuck him that day because otherwise he would've taken the pen. But afterwards, I went straight to the police station and filed a report. I got a judge to give me the restraining order, but they didn't prosecute the ass-hole. The cops look after each other in this town."

Axel says, "That's unbelievable. Somebody should lock that guy up!"

Axel's wheels are turning; He'd been considering aborting his plan to kill Brooke because of Craig, but now he's develop-ing an ingenious plan.

Brooke walks into the kitchen to get drinks for the two of them.

Vicky's now in the living room with Axel. They give each other a look like they know what the other's thinking. It's bril-liant. Vicky steps into the bedroom, out of sight.

Axel calls out, "Hey Brooke, I really think it'd be best if you reported that that cop was here... sitting on your doorstep... waiting for you. If you were alone... if I wasn't here, who knows what he had planned for you... He seems like a dangerous guy."

She walks back into the living room with the drinks and re-sponds, "I would report it, but they won't do anything about it."

Axel picks up her phone, "I insist, just get it on record. I'm sure he'll be reprimanded, and that might keep him away for a while..."

Brooke is hesitant, so Axel adds, "Do it for me, please, so that I don't worry about you later."

Brooke says, "You are SO sweet," and hesitantly makes the call. It's now on record that Officer Craig was here this evening against Brooke's wishes.

Brooke says, "Sorry about this whole scene. You're paying for a good time, and I want you to have a good night. How can I make this up to you?" She wraps her arms around Axel's shoulders and kisses his neck.

Axel responds, "Well, I wasn't going to ask, but I kinda like sex a little rough. I have a paddle in my car. I would love to spank you with it?"

Brook complies, "I normally don't do that, but considering everything that's happened tonight, you can spank me some… But not really hard!"

Axel walks back to his car and retrieves his bag that has the paddle in it. When he returns, Brook is already in the bedroom stripped down to nothing but sheer light blue bra and panties. Axel puts his bag down, opens his wallet and peels off $500.00, and puts it on the bedroom window sill.

Axel opens his bag, pulls out the paddle and leans it against the bed. He approaches Brooke who's standing in the middle of the bedroom. Axel brushes her hair to the side and kisses her neck. As he does this, he undoes her bra, and it drops to the ground. Axel kneels down, kisses her stomach, and pulls her panties to the ground. He leads her to the bed and has her lay down on her belly so she is ass-up. He smacks her ass a couple times with the paddle. Vicky is in the room watching; she's ab-

56

solutely giddy. Vicky tells Axel to fuck Brooke doggie style. So Axel lays the paddle flat on the bed, takes off his clothes, and puts on a condom. He mounts Brooke and starts giving it to her hard and fast. He looks down at her ass and can see traces of the white hearts left by the paddle that are surrounded by redness.

Vicky is sadistically loving all of this. She commands, "We're gonna donkey punch this bitch." Axel, still fucking away, asks quietly, "What?" He's heard that term before but doesn't know what it means.

Vicky explains, "A donkey punch is when you're fucking a chick doggie style - much like you are doing at this very moment - and you punch her in the back of the head, like you might punch a donkey you were riding… donkey punch… But since we're homicidal killers, instead of your fist, we're going to use that thick-ass piece of wood with the loving heart cut-out."

Axel looks to the paddle lying on the bed and then looks to the back of Brooke's head, which is bouncing forward and back. He nods in agreement and gives Vicky a little smile. Brooke is faced forward, holding herself up in doggie style. Axel's doing most of the work, thrusting into her, but he says, "I need a break. You do the work for a while." Axel holds still, and she starts bumping, back and forth and grinding, taking his cock in and out. She's good, and she seems to be really enjoying the sex.

Axel slowly reaches and picks up the paddle. He holds it up like a baseball bat, with his hands up by his face. He's about to swing and Vicky grabs the paddle to stop him for a moment. She wants in on it. She presses her chest to Axel's back and wraps her arms around Axel's arms. Both of her hands are overtop of Axel's hands on the paddle. She wants to feel the swing and the connection.

Meanwhile, Brooke, completely unaware of what is going on behind her, now appears to be building herself to an orgasm. Vicky whispers to let her finish. Axle and Vicky watch and wait patiently, with the paddle cocked back like a baseball bat, for the next 30 seconds or so. Brooke works it faster and faster and has a rather intense and vocal orgasm. Then, as she winds down her body's sexual motions, Axel and Vicky pull the paddle back just a little farther and swing away at the side of Brooke's blonde head.

On contact, there's a loud 'CRACK.' Brooke collapses to the bed. Her skull is definitely fractured, there's blood spilling from the side of her head, and she's not moving... But she is still breathing. Axel says to Vicky, "I hope she stays alive for a minute." He gets up and flushes the condom three times and puts on his clothes. He gets out his camera and rushes to take his 'before' picture before she dies.

He opens his bag and asks Vicky her preference. She pulls out a piece of rope. Axel puts on latex gloves and wraps the rope around Brooke's neck and squeezes until she's dead.

Vicky gets an even sicker, more twisted thought, "Axel, you know CPR, right? ... What if you revived her? ... We could strangle her again!"

58

Axel smiles at the depravity of that notion, but tells her, "Too much work, and we've got a lot to do tonight... Plus, if we revive her, she still won't be conscious."

Axel takes Brooke's fingerprints with blood from her head and takes his 'after' picture. He cleans up any trace that he was there that evening, including cleaning Brooke's neck and belly where he kissed her. He doesn't usually kiss them; maybe Vicky's desires are rubbing off on him? ...He takes his $500.00 back and finds another $385.00 in her purse.

He explains to Vicky: "Officer Craig looks SOMEWHAT guilty from Brooke's 9-1-1 call and restraining order, but that's not quite good enough."

Axel, wearing his latex gloves, goes to Brooke's kitchen looking for something... not quite sure what ... Perfect! He finds a shot glass in the cupboard. Then he finds baggies in a drawer. He goes to her bathroom and takes a couple Q-tips. He goes back to Brooke's body and scoops up some blood into the shot glass and seals the shot glass into a baggie ... thinks twice and puts that baggie into a second baggie - just to be safe. Vicky watches on curiously.

They leave Brooke's apartment (10:20pm) and drive back to Axel's house. Axel pulls out the bag that was returned to him from the police the day he got out of jail. Recall that Officer Craig handled several items before putting on latex gloves. In particular, he handled the fingerprint paper and a large hunting knife! Both items do not have Axel's fingerprints... But they do have Craig's fingerprints! Once Craig handled the items, they were put in a bag, and when they were examined, no other bare fingers would have touched them. And Craig's fingerprints wouldn't have been wiped off!

Axel only removes the fingerprint paper from his bag and leaves everything else, including that knife. Vicky inquires, "You know… Craig's fingerprints are on the knife… Shouldn't we plant that!? …If you stick that knife into Brooke and leave it, that'll lead the cops right to Craig."

She thinks she's said something brilliant that Axel didn't think of, but Axel explains, "If I plant that knife, you're right, it does have Craig's fingerprints. But it's a very distinct looking knife, and the police processed it in my arrest a couple weeks ago. I signed their release paperwork to get it back. Someone who processed the knife will remember it. This same knife at the crime scene, even with Craig's fingerprints, makes me a suspect too, especially once Craig starts accusing me. I have a better plan than that..."

Vicky is intrigued and she watches as Axel goes to under his floorboard to his collection. He adds Brooke's fingerprints and pictures to the binder and removes three pages three previous victims in LA. He's somewhat saddened to give up these possessions, but sacrifices must be made for freedom.

He's probably touched the pages with his bare fingers, so, wearing gloves, he wipes down the fingerprint pages and pictures with a damp cloth. He was going to plant these pages intact, but Vicky gives him a better idea:

"Keep the 'after' pictures, and cut the fingerprint pages in half... You can keep one picture and the right or left hand worth of prints for your collection."

What a great idea! This cheers Axel up. He starts to see real value in having Vicky as a partner after all.

Axel goes online to a website that, for $19.99, gives him a background check on Officer Craig Carter. He gets Craig's home address, home phone number, cell phone number and some background info. Part of what he learns is that Craig is never married and does not have kids. Therefore, it's likely he lives alone.

Axel drives back to Brooke's apartment, parks down the street, and walks over to her door. He opens the door with his shirt over his hands, and once inside, puts back on his latex gloves. He takes out the blank fingerprint paper that has Craig's prints and takes a set of blood fingerprints from Brooke (right hand only). Axel leaves her fingers bloody this time...

Axel calls Craig from one of his unregistered cell phones (11:05 pm). Craig isn't a genius, but he is not stupid either.
Axel: "Hi Craig, it's your old friend Axel."
Craig: "Axel?... What the hell do you want? How did you get this number?"

Axel: "...You were right about me Craig. I'm a BAAAD guy. But I found out, you're not so nice either... blackmail for sex, violating a restraining order, shame on you!... ...When you left, I took Brooke for a little drive. We'll be in Victorville in about 10 minutes."

(Victorville is a town about 80 miles east of LA in the middle of the desert).

Craig: "What the fuck! Is this a game to you?"

Axel: "Just listen Craig... If you want to come and save Brooke, she promised she'd give you a few more freebees... Or maybe you just want to stop me and be the big hero... But you should know, the last thing she did before we left was report that you violated your restraining order... ...Meet me off the first exit in Victorville. There's a Denny's there. I will call on the payphone in exactly 90 minutes with more information. That'll be exactly 12:35am... And Craig, this little game is just for us. I could be watching from anywhere. If any other cops show up, Brooke disappears into the desert, I leave the country, and you'll have some explaining to do about breaking the restraining order and being the last person to have seen Brooke alive..."

Axel hangs up before Craig can respond. He knows Craig will do what he was told. Vicky comments, "Impressive... You just got Craig to voluntarily drive an hour and a half into the middle of nowhere, just so he wouldn't be in our way."

Ten minutes later Axel and Vicky drive past Craig's home, and see that all the lights are off. They park a block down the

62

street. Nobody seemed to be there, but in case Craig has a roommate or girlfriend, Axel dials Craig's home phone number. It rings four times and then voicemail. Axel goes to the front door and rings the doorbell with his knuckle. He's satisfied that nobody's there.

Axel walks around to the back door and puts on latex gloves. He looks at the lock and thinks, 'Oh my god, this guy's a cop, and all he has on his door for protection is a Wellington basic lock.' Axel is able to pick the lock in seconds and enters.

Let's see, where's a good hiding place … Can't be too obvious or Craig will find it before the cops investigate. Can't be too hidden, or these dumb-ass lazy cops may not find it at all. Ah, heating duct. It's springtime, so he won't be using the heater anytime soon.

Axel unscrews the heating vent cover and places up there:

1) Bloody fingerprints from Brooke

2) The rope he used to strangle Brooke

3) Bloody fingerprints and 'before' pictures of three other victims

Axel replaces the vent cover and looks around for more nails to hammer into Craig's proverbial coffin. He goes to the kitchen and notices a set of knives in a wooden block. He takes one (of the six) steak knives from the block. It's a sturdy knife with a sharp point. He goes through Craig's bedroom and closet sensing he might find one more item… Ah, a baseball bat, perfect!

Axel next takes out the baggies containing the shot glass of Brooke's blood. The blood has spilled out of the shot glass, but is contained in the baggie. Axel dips a Q-tip into the blood and leaves just a small dab on the heating vent cover. He puts a small dab on the wall at eye level under the vent cover, and a dab on the kitchen counter by the set of knives...

Now it's back to Brooke's place for the final time.

Brooke's head wound is from a flat paddle with an edge. The baseball bat wouldn't match... so Axel makes it match. With latex gloves on, he strikes Brooke with the bat to her existing head wound ...four, five, six times, as hard as he can. Her skull is crushed in, badly. There are brains mixed in with the fragmented pieces of skull. Now, there will be no definitive way to tell this bat was not the only object to smash her head.

Axel takes Craig's steak knife and thrusts it into Brooke's chest, in between ribs, and into her heart.

This trip was messy. Good thing Axel brought another change of clothes. As he leaves Brooke's apartment, he positions the door just slightly ajar.

Axel drives to a payphone and calls 9-1-1 (11:50pm). He knows the call will be recorded, so he talks in a high pitched tone and uses an English accent to disguise his voice. He gives Brooke's address and says, "I heard a woman screaming for her life. She was calling out for help and screaming, 'Craig, don't hurt me!'" ... And Axel hangs up before they can ask him any questions.

Axel heads home to start a cozy fire in his fireplace and burn the paddle and bloodstained clothes and all of the other evidence. He's truly proud of his plan and his execution (execution of the plan, not the girl ... although that was good too).

Craig should be getting to Victorville soon... I wonder if there is a Denny's at the first offramp?

This whole plan is contingent on cops following easy clues and doing their job. The waiting is truly nerve-racking; Axel doesn't like to leave even the simplest of tasks in someone else's hands. But as long as the police respond to the 9-1-1 call, they will find the body, the bat, and the knife. They surely have to realize that Brooke had a restraining order against Craig. They will run the prints on the bat and match them to Craig, who should already be the primary suspect now because of Brooke's phone call to the police. Craig won't have an alibi for most of the night because he drove to Victorville alone. This will be enough evidence for a search warrant of Craig's house. Once there, they should easily see that the knife in Brooke's heart is part of Craig's knife set. Looking further at Craig's house, they will find traces of Brooke's blood, Brooke's murder weapon (rope), Brooke's blood fingerprints WITH Craig's own fingerprints on the paper, AND enough evidence from THREE other murders in LA to convict Craig as a serial killer.

Now if a guy this guilty says he saw me with Brooke last night at her apartment, would you believe him???

This whole plan will come together, but Axel knows he has to go about his life like nothing ever happened. But naturally, he's anxious. Axel has trouble falling asleep that night. But he manages a couple hours sleep before his alarm clock goes off for work. As he wakes up, he smells coffee. He proceeds to the kitchen, and discovers that Vicky had prepared breakfast for the both of them: eggs, bacon, pancakes, fresh squeezed orange juice. He asks, "Where did you get this stuff?"

Vicky replies, "I got up early and went to the grocery store silly… Do you think I crapped out the eggs myself?"

Axel replies, "I hadn't considered that… but you ARE full of surprises." Axel digs in to the breakfast. It's exceptionally good! He's somewhat confused; he didn't know Vicky, (a ghost, or whatever she was), could do this. But the food was real – he's stuffed.

Chapter 5

(M)eat The Smiths

The locksmith shop gets a call from a customer in Beverly Hills, Mrs. Smith. She needs all the locks at her house re-keyed. Axel is dispatched in the company van; Vicky tags along. They arrive at a beautiful house in a beautiful neighborhood, probably worth at least ten million dollars. Mrs. Smith answers the door; she's holding back a rottweiler who seems friendly at first.

Mrs. Smith is a beautiful woman: about 30, long blonde hair, and a great rack… big, but not too big for her frame (probably fake though - she has way too much money for them not to be surgically enhanced). Axel's in his uniform, so she's expecting him. She says not to worry about Jake (the dog). Jake is calm as Axel puts his hand out to introduce himself. Jake sniffs and licks his hand, and Mrs. Smith says, "Now he'll be your friend forever." Axel comes inside.

But Jake quickly starts growling and barking fiercely in Vicky's direction as she tries to enter the house. Mrs. Smith apologizes and puts the dog in a separate room.

As she shows Axel the five exterior doors around the house, Mrs. Smith explains, "We'd been having jewelry and silverware and little things around the house disappear. The last straw though was brazen when a $25,000 painting disappeared off the living room wall. So we had to fire everyone who works in the house: the butler, the maid, the cook, and the gardener. The servant's quarters are empty, just me and my husband in this large house for now. We'll be re-hiring soon, but they all had keys to the house, so that's why we need everything re-keyed... Here's the security alarm station. If you need the code to re-do the locks, it's 8-7-6-5-4."

It is amazing how trusting people are of strangers in uniforms! This wasn't an unusual exchange. Axel is often given people's vital information freely.

Mrs. Smith retires to another part of the house, out of sight, and Axel starts on the locks. Vicky was immediately struck by Mrs. Smith, another blonde, and just her type. Vicky: "I like her."

Axel" "No!"

Vicky: "I want her."

Axel" "No way!"

Vicky: "... The dog is put away. We're all alone with her in this big house. We could go have some fun with her right now!... And I bet there's a safe somewhere with lots of cash."

Axel: "No! We don't EVER kill customers... It'd be stupid. It would make an easy pattern that would lead the cops right to me."

Vicky knows he's right, but she WANTS her.

Vicky: "If you kill only one customer, there's no pattern at all. No reason for the police to investigate a locksmith that only had an hour of contact with the victim. I'd say that a recently fired maid, cook, gardener or BUTLER would be a much more likely suspect... Think about it."

Axel: "We definitely can't do it now, people know I'm here."

Vicky: "That's the spirit. Let's come back tonight then."

Axel: "The husband will be here, I don't do the whole home invasion thing. It's too risky."

Vicky: "After what you pulled off last night... You can't just go back to killing hookers. That's child's play. You NEED to take it to the next level. You can do this! ...Do it for me."

Axel finishes the job at this house and goes back to the locksmith shop. He's still mulling over Vicky's request. It feels like a bad idea, but Axel kept an extra key to the Smith house for himself... just in case he changes his mind.

After work, Axel is exhausted from lack of sleep and takes a nap. When he wakes, Vicky has prepared dinner. It's a feast of steak and mashed potatoes and creamed spinach and fresh rolls she baked herself. Axel enjoys the meal and it helps nudge him to a decision. He tells Vicky, he's decided to give her ... Mrs. Smith ... this evening. Vicky is very pleased.

Axel packs a special bag of supplies. They wait until the middle of the night and drive to the Smith neighborhood. To be discreet, they have to park and walk for about a half mile since the houses are so far apart. At the Smith driveway, Axel whispers to Vicky, "Wait here. Meet me upstairs once I've got every-thing under control." He doesn't want Jake to see her.

Axel enters through a side door. Jake comes running over, but he recognizes Axel's scent and doesn't bark. Axel pets Jake and leads him to the closest door he comes to; it's a bathroom. He closes the door, and the dog remains calm in the dark. He should go to sleep, Axel thinks/hopes.

This took only maybe 10 seconds, and Axel figures he has about 20 more seconds to disable the alarm. He gets to the alarm station … 8-7-6-5-4 … disarmed. The house is completely quiet. The Smiths must be sound asleep. Axel puts on latex gloves and wipes off everything he's already touched. (He needed a bare hand to greet the dog).

Axel has procured some chloroform. He takes it out and douses a rag as he stalks up the spiral staircase towards the mas-ter bedroom. He slowly opens the bedroom door and sees Mrs. and Mr. Smith asleep in their bed. Axel has a gun ready in his pocket in case he can't pull this off. If EITHER wake up before he sedates BOTH of them, this may get tricky. He covers Mr. Smith's face first, gently holding the rag over his nose and mouth. Mr. Smith never opens his eyes. That was easy!

Axel now moves over to Mrs. Smith and gently covers her nose and mouth with the rag… But her eyes open immediately, and she starts to struggle! Axel holds the cloth more firmly to her face and she drifts back to sleep in a couple seconds.

Axel has some time to set up shop. "Vicky, it's clear now."

She appears, "See, isn't this fun?"

Axel is enjoying this, but he doesn't admit it to Vicky.

The master bedroom that he's preparing is giant sized. The bed is huge; there's a sitting area within the bedroom with a couch and chairs, and a full entertainment system with a giant tv. Axel brings over a chair from the sitting area puts it at the foot of the bed to the left corner. He puts Mr. Smith in the chair and uses rope to thoroughly tie his chest and waist to the back of the chair. He thoroughly ties his legs to the chair's legs. And then he handcuffs Mr. Smith's hands to each other in his lap.

Mr. Smith is at least 50 years old and scrawny – not much of a challenge if he somehow gets loose. Clearly, his fine, piece of ass, wife married him for his money.

Axel removes the covers from the bed. Mrs. Smith is wearing a thin silky red nightgown. It extends to about her knees, and the way it drapes over and conforms to the curves of her motionless body is very sexy. He leaves her laying face-up, and uses more rope to tie her right arm to the left edge of the bedpost, and her left arm to the middle of the bedpost (it's a huge bed; if he went to the other edge of the bedpost, she'd be completely stretched out). There's some play in the rope for her to move her arms a little, but her hands will remain above her head. Axel leaves Mrs. Smith's legs unrestrained.

He finds a small table in a hallway and brings it into the master bedroom. It is a fancy wood table that's just about 1 foot

71

deep and 3 feet wide. They were using it to rest a vase on. Axel is using it to spread his tools onto.

He lays out for them to see: six different cutting devices (from large knives to a surgical scalpel), acetylene blowtorch, needle nose pliers, a pair of gardening clippers, and an empty grocery-sized paper bag that's expanded open on the table. This last item is just because Axel finds it amusing to leave them questioning to themselves what horrible surprise could be in there… and he's sure that thought will cross their minds.

Killing is the orgasm – the money shot. But inflicting terror and pain is the foreplay and the fornication. His victims' terror and pain feeds Axel's sense of power. Death brings it all to a climax, but death is also a release – a release of power, since death relinquishes all of his victims' terror and pain. Like sex, it's not just about the destination, it's about the journey.

Axel lights the blowtorch in preparation for the Smiths' arrival to consciousness. He looks to Vicky, "Anything requests?"

Vicky can sense that Axel is at the height of his game, and doesn't interfere with any suggestions. So they wait for the Smiths to awaken.

Mr. Smith starts to lift his head a little. Axel, holding the torch up in one hand, grabs Mr. Smith's face with his other hand and squeezes his cheeks in. He looks him in the eyes and says, "If you say a word or make a sound, I'll burn your wife's cunt."

Mrs. Smith opens her eyes a minute later. Axel holds a hand over her mouth and makes a similar threat to her about her husband's eye. She's clearly panicked, but stays quiet as Axel removes his hand… But her husband, upon seeing her awake and frightened, blurts out in a timid voice, "We'll be fine honey… I love you."

Axel gives him a dirty look, grabs his wife's ankle that's closest to her husband (maybe 2 feet from Mr. Smith) and swipes the blowtorch across her calf. She lets out a little high pitched scream that she does her best to squelch. It leaves an ugly burn mark about 4 inches long, and it gives off a disturbing smell of burning flesh.

Mr. Smith starts to cry a little. There are tears in the wife's eyes too.

Axel says to the wife, "You may now speak if you'd like to address your husband's stupidity."

She says, "I love you too. Please don't talk."

Axel expected venom and proclaims, "I'm touched. I figured you as a trophy wife that hated her husband… …Back to quiet time."

Axel's mind is churning. He'll play with this concept later.

First financial business, "If you both do exactly as you're told, you might live through this. If not, I will NOT kill you quickly, I will burn, cut and dismember you in front of each other…"

He pauses to let it sink in, "There IS a safe in this house. Where is it, and what's the combination?…"

No answer.

"You can both speak when asked a question from me…
Where is it?!"

Axel approaches the wife with the blowtorch in his hand. He
looks over to the husband. Axel lifts Mrs. Smith's nightgown
just a little to expose her thigh and moves the flame to a few
inches from her thigh. "Mr. Smith, tell me about the safe or
you're going to smell your wife's flesh burning again… Three
… Two …"

Mr. Smith succumbs, "Wait!… …It's behind the picture of
the sailboat right there." He motions his head and hands to the
picture that's very close - behind him and to his right."

Axel extinguishes the blowtorch, rests it with his other tools
on the table, and removes the picture from the wall. "Excellent
safe." Axel knows from safes since he's a locksmith. "This
would take me days to get into it if you didn't give me the combination, nice selection... The combination please!…"

Mr. Smith gives Axel the combination and Axel puts a rag in
Mr. Smith's mouth to gag him. "You do NOT want to remove
this gag." Axel knows Mr. Smith could lift his arms and remove
it, but he won't, he's way too scared. Axel says to the wife, "No
talking for you either Mrs. Smith," but leaves her mouth free.

Axel opens the safe, and he turns and smiles at Vicky; there
must be $50,000 in cash! He puts it all in his bag. He also sees
jewelry, probably another $50,000 worth. He asks Vicky, "Do
you want any of this jewelry?" Axel has no desire to try to sell

it; that might get him caught. Vicky says she doesn't want it either. So they leave the jewelry in the safe.

But there's one more item in the safe: a semi-automatic hand gun, loaded. Axel takes it out and you can almost see a light bulb appear and turn on over his head... "Vicky, I have an idea. I'll let you in on it soon… But first, didn't you want to play with Mrs. Smith?"

Axel pulls over another chair from the sitting area and sits down next to Mr. Smith at the foot of the bed. He's intentionally tied Mr. Smith in a way so that his body is restrained and his hands are handcuffed to each other, but his arms can move freely. Axel wants to see if he'll even try to fight. It would be futile, but providing this slight temptation is a power play and no real perceived risk for Axel.

Vicky approaches the bed and says, "Axel, I want you to cut the nightgown off her for me."

Axel stands, grabs the material at both of her breasts, and pulls apart. The nightgown rips in between her breasts and straight down to her waist. Her body is jolted a little and her exposed breasts jiggle for a moment on her chest. Axel grabs the material at her waist and pulls apart again, and it's torn all the way down the middle. There are only thin straps of red material left on her shoulders and the rest of the nightgown is beneath her and to her sides on the bed. She has panties on, but Axel rips them right off too. What a body! Axel returns to his seat next to the gagged Mr. Smith.

Vicky strips down, naked, and climbs onto the bed with Mrs. Smith. She lies on top of her. Vicky kisses her neck. Then she drifts upward to nibble on her ear. And then she kisses Mrs. Smith on the lips. All the while, she has her left hand on Mrs. Smith's right breast, alternating between grabbing the flesh with her whole hand, and squeezing her nipples with her thumb and forefinger. Mrs. Smith is just laying there, motionless, silent, being groped.

Vicky slides down a little. The hand that was on Mrs. Smith's breast moves to Mrs. Smith's clit, and Vicky's mouth moves to her left nipple. She bites the nipple, hard, but doesn't get any reaction from Mrs. Smith. After a little of this, Vicky slides all the way down to eat her pussy... But Mrs. Smith's knees are closed and Vicky can't spread them. Axel sees this and commands, "Spread your legs... Do it now!"

Mrs. Smith, frightened, spreads her legs far apart, and Vicky begins licking her pussy. Vicky hums and moans, but still no reaction from Mrs. Smith. She just looks petrified.

Axel breaks his gaze on the action for just a moment and nudges the gagged Mr. Smith with his elbow, "This is hot, right?!... Vicky, eating out your wife. They're both so fuckin' hot!"

But there's no response from the confused looking man that can't speak.

After a while of this, Vicky looks up at Mrs. Smith from between her legs and says, "My turn."

Vicky stands on the bed, walks forward two steps and gets on her knees over Mrs. Smith so that her pussy is in Mrs. Smith's face. But Mrs. Smith just lays there. Axel commands, "Mrs. Smith... eat Vicky's pussy!"

Mrs. Smith looks at Axel and says, "I don't know how to do that?"

Axel says, "Just stick your tongue out and lick... You'll do fine."

Mrs. Smith, obviously terrified says, "I really don't know what you mean. I want to do it, really. Please explain better."

Axel approaches her at the bedside, "Just stick out your tongue and lick." He does the motion in the air himself to show her – he sticks out his tongue and moves his tongue and chin, out and up a few times. "Feel free to do circles and X's with your tongue too... Got it?"

Vicky's pussy is still right there waiting, and Mrs. Smith follows the instructions she was given. She licks Vicky's pussy. Vicky loves it! She builds to three climaxes and is completely satisfied after about ten minutes. Vicky collapses on the bed next to Mrs. Smith and rests there for several seconds, breathing heavily.

With one part frustration and two parts puzzlement, Axel says, ***"You can stop licking now Mrs. Smith."***

Vicky gives Mrs. Smith a sweet little kiss on the lips, gets up, gets dressed, and sits on the couch across the room.

Axel announces, "I was genuinely touched with your displays of affection for each other earlier, Smiths. And I've been wondering: just how much you two do actually love each other. So I've thought up some games for us to test it out…"

Axel picks up his camera and the Smiths' gun and walks over to Mrs. Smith's bedside. He puts the camera down on the nightstand there and asks, "Mrs. Smith, would you suck my dick to stop me from shooting your husband?" He points the gun at the silenced Mr. Smith, who begins to sob again.

Axel doesn't get an answer immediately, so he cocks the gun – 'shick shick'. Mrs. Smith blurts out, "Wait!... I'll do it."

Axel gets a knife and cuts her left arm free so that only her right arm is tied to the closest part of the bedpost. Axel tells her, "You don't have to do this. I can just kill him… But if you decide to bite me, there's not an item on that table that won't mutilate every inch of you body… inside and out. And I know how to keep you alive while doing it... Understand?"

She nods 'yes'. Then, just to amuse himself, Axel addresses the gagged Mr. Smith, "You have a very loving wife here. If at any time you don't approve of what's going on, just say 'dragon'."

Vicky gets a good laugh out of that, and Axel also chuckles.

Before anything else, Axel picks up his camera and takes a picture of Mrs. Smith on the bed: her 'before' picture.

Axel removes his shirt, undoes his jeans, and takes his penis out. Mrs. Smith gets on her knees on the floor with her right hand still up, attached to the bedpost. She takes Axel's cock in her mouth. Axel says, "Wait a second, look up at me," and takes a POV picture looking downward with his dick in her mouth. He has a purpose for this.

Axel expects she will just take it partly in her mouth and be lazy, so he's waiting to give commands like: 'move faster' or 'take it deeper'. But she does it well right away... very well actually; it's a great blowjob. She obviously doesn't want to be reprimanded, so she's very diligent and compliant. And she has a skill for it.

Axel enjoys it for a few minutes and then decides to torment the husband while the wife is still going to town on him: "I can see why you married this one... God that is good... Does she still suck your dick like this? ...You're married, she can't possibly still suck your dick anymore..."

Looking down at the wife, "Do you suck your husband's dick?"

She stops, frees her mouth, and answers, "Yes."

Axel asks, "How often? Just birthdays and holidays, right?"

She replies, "Not very often, maybe every other month or so."

Axel says, "Ok, keep sucking."

She begins felating him again, and Axel speaks while she works, "If you really love the guy, a guy who provides such a beautiful house and all the trimmings, you should be doing this

79

for him every night. Will you appreciate him after tonight and do this every night for him?"

She nods 'yes' without stopping what she is doing... Axel continues, "You're a lucky man Mr. Smith."

A minute later, Axel again addresses Mr. Smith, who is forced to watch the back of his wife's head bobbing at Axel's pelvis, "Mr. Smith, the question now is… Do YOU love your wife enough to suck my dick?"

Mr. Smith's eyes get wide. Axel pauses and laughs, "Just kidding, I'm not gay... Gotcha!"

After ten minutes, Axel doesn't cum, but he's satisfied. He tells Mrs. Smith to lie back down on the bed, and he redoes his jeans and puts on his shirt. "Excellent, Mrs. Smith, you passed the first test. You must really love your husband. I'm gonna tie you up better for this next test."

He secures both her wrists and both ankles to the bed with rope, again face up, and puts a rag in her mouth. Axel picks up a pen and pad of paper from the nightstand and hands them to Mr. Smith and commands "Write 'My wife is…' and finish the sentence in your own words. Then sign the paper at the VERY BOTTOM."

Mr. Smith begins writing. His wrists are handcuffed, but he can still awkwardly use his hands. Axel takes a mental note that he's left handed (this is important). Axel takes the pad back from Mr. Smith and reads out loud, "My wife is… beautiful and wonderful and I hope she knows she is the love of my life... Signed Eugene Smith."

This triggers Mrs. Smith's emotions and she begins to cry harder than she has all evening. This triggers Mr. Smith to weep more also.

Axel says, "That is truly beautiful… Now take the pad and pen and add to it: '…But she is a cheating whore."

Mr. Smith's facial expression turns from emotional sadness to outrage and concern. He takes the paper and pen in his hand, but he does not write. Axel gets impatient, "Should I light up the blowtorch again? … But…She…Is…A…Cheating…Whore!"

Mr. Smith writes the words begrudgingly. Axel explains, "That was not really the test." He takes the pen and paper and picks up the garden clippers from the table. They're the type of hand tool with a curved blade that's used for cutting tree branches of up to about an inch thick. He hands the tool to the husband and pushes his chair about two feet forward so that he's at the corner of the bed next to his wife's foot. Axel inquires, "Mr. Smith... Would you cut off your wife's pinky toe… to save her life?"

Axel paces the room and gives him about 30 seconds to consider. Then he picks up the gun and points it at Mrs. Smith's chest. It's a good thing she's gagged, because in this 30 seconds, she's hysterical - crying and trying to scream through her gag. But with the gun now pointed at her, she knows what must be done. Though she can't talk and can't move her limbs much, with the little bit of play she has from the rope, she points her toes out toward her husband, like an offering. She doesn't want to be executed.

Mr. Smith has the tool in his left hand and slowly inserts his wife's piggy toe into the cutting area between the metal. He looks to his wife who has tears streaming down her face. She's nodding up and down to relieve his hesitation. Mr. Smith closes his eyes and squeezes the handles together. There is a sickening metal through bone sound, and the piggy toe drops to the ground.

His wife's screams of agony are mostly absorbed by the rag. There's blood... lots of blood. Axel lights the blowtorch and swipes it by the stump to cauterize the wound and stop the bleeding. But this is even more painful than the cutting for Mrs. Smith, and she's clearly in agony.

Vicky watches on, mesmerized at this performance by Axel.

Axel says, "Last test... Mr. Smith, I now know that you'd cut off one of your wife's toes to save HER life... Would you cut off her second toe to save YOUR OWN life?"

That cranked up the panic level in the room somehow even further. Mrs. Smith is already in so much pain, and the husband feels so much sympathy and guilt.

But Axel doesn't wait very long for an answer. After just a few seconds, Axel approaches Mr. Smith's LEFT side, kneels down, holds the gun to his LEFT temple at a slight upward direction, and fires...

82

Blood and brains and skull pieces spray out the other side of his head. Mr. Smith's head falls forward, as far as the ropes will allow. Mrs. Smith is struggling as hard as she can and screaming through her gag - like a dog that's had its vocal chords removed.

Axel verbalizes his plan in retrospect to Vicky, so that Mrs. Smith can enjoy it also. As he packs his bag he explains:

"Once I saw the gun in the safe, my mind went straight to murder/suicide between husband and wife. We're leaving the jewelry locked up in the safe, and we won't remove anything else from the house, except for the cash... I would assume nobody else but the Smith's knows about that cash. And there's no forced entry, so it's not a robbery.

The picture of Mrs. Smith sucking an anonymous dick, obviously not her husband's, and his creepy note, in his own handwriting, is proof that she was cheating on him. And that's motive for him to kill her. Hell, it's almost a confession to killing her. He tied her up, and burnt her leg, and cut off her toe... before shooting her three times - the sick bastard! ...I'll be leaving the garden clippers and blowtorch here, both with his fingerprints." Axel wraps Mr. Smith's LEFT hand around the blowtorch and sets it on the floor.

Axel continues, "Mr. Smith needs to have gunshot residue on his hands in order to have killed himself and his wife so..." Axel unties the now dead Mr. Smith, lifts him up, and rests most of his weight on his knees on the bed. He puts the gun in his dead LEFT hand and points it at his wife's chest. She's well aware of her fate. Axel manipulates Mr. Smith's finger and fires three times... Mrs. Smith is dead. Axel leaves Mr. Smith's gun in Mr. Smith's left hand.

Now the clock is ticking. A neighbor surely heard the four total gunshots. Axel quickly takes his after picture of Mrs. Smith. He feels that he only has time to fingerprint one hand, so he unties her left wrist, dips her fingers in a gunshot wound, and fingerprints her. Instead of cleaning up her fingers, he wipes blood all over her whole hand and leaves her hand on top of a wound – now it doesn't look odd that her hand is bloody.

Axel puts on clean latex gloves and does one last check of the room to make sure he's not leaving behind anything that he hasn't planted. He tells Vicky to meet him at the car and heads downstairs. He opens the bathroom door to let Jake out, "Good dog... OK... Jake, I'm not sure when anyone will be by here to take care of you, *but there's water in the toilet... and feel free to eat the Smiths if you get hungry.*"

Axel re-sets the house alarm and leaves through the side door. He locks the door behind him with his key, and jogs to his car with his bag, now a little heavier with cash. No cops in sight yet, but in this neighborhood, they'll be along soon. As he starts the car and pulls onto the street, he hears the sirens and watches three cop cars speed past him in the opposite direction, going toward the Smith house.

When Axel gets home, he files away his pictures and finger-prints and counts the money. He was pretty far off in his estimate – there was $80,000 there!

The next day after work, Axel turns on the evening news. He loves the evening news; they talk about his works all the time. He's curious about what may be reported about the Smiths AND Brooke. Nothing about Brooke tonight, but he does get…

"Top story tonight… Police have concluded that Doctor Eugene Smith violently murdered his wife, Brenda Smith, in their Beverly Hills estate late last night, and then turned the gun on himself after finding out she cheated on him with an un-known man. All acquaintances we interviewed described Mr. Smith as a gentle, loving husband and are in shock that he could have done something like this… In other news…"

Chapter 6

Craig's Perspective

So, after Brooke's murder, the next day and a half went splendidly for Axel. But Officer Craig didn't fare so well. He got the call from Axel at 11:05pm. He grabs his gun and badge and is out the door for Victorville within a few minutes. While driving, Craig calls his partner, Megan, on his cell phone:

Craig: "Megan, we were right about Axel."

Megan: "What's going on?"

Craig: "He either kidnapped or already murdered Brooke."

Megan: "Brooke? …The hooker you were bangin' who got the restraining order against you?"

Craig: "Yea, her... I was following Axel. He picked her up off Sunset and they went to her place. I tried to warn her, but she wouldn't listen. That was about an hour and a half ago."

Megan: "OK, we already knew the guy likes hookers, what else happened?"

Craig: "That bold mother-fucker just called my cell phone and told me he abducted her - that they'd be in Victorville, and I had to go out there alone and meet him... He knows about my restraining order and thinks he can kill her and blame it on me… He's watched way too many bad movies."

Megan: "What're you gonna to do?"

Craig: "I'm not sure yet, but I just left my house, and I'm on my way out there. I know he's gotta have some kind of ridiculous scheme planned to bring me all the way out to Victorville, but that's all I know. I'll have to play it by ear."

Megan: "I think you should call Victorville P.D. If Brooke's life is in danger, they're closer and you shouldn't be doing this without back-up."

Craig: "Axel said he'll be watching and if other cops show up, he'll just kill her and take off. That part I think he'll do. My best chance of catching him is to play along for now."

Megan: "Alright, then I'm coming with you."

Craig: "I'm already on my way. Plus, he gave me a deadline to make, and I think if I don't follow his rules, I won't get a shot at him. But, I could use your help with this... I'll keep my cell phone on speaker when I meet with Axel. Just stay silent and listen. That way, if I get into any trouble, you'll know what's going on, and you can call in for backup if I need it."

Megan: "OK, I'll call Victorville P.D. now. I won't tell them everything, but I'll make sure they have a few units ready to respond to a kidnapping and homicide suspect."

Craig: "Good... One other thing... do a check and see if Axel has any history around Victorville. If he has any previous addresses or known associates out there, you can have the Victorville P.D. check those locations."

Megan: "I'm on it... ...Craig, be careful."

About a half hour later, Megan calls back. She's alerted Victorville P.D., but there's no history for Axel around that area.

Craig gets to the first exit in Victorville at 12:35am and has Megan on the phone, "Megan, there doesn't seem to be a Denny's right here. I'm gonna to proceed to the next off ramp. Look up where the closest Denny's is for me."

She does the research on her computer and replies, "There is no Denny's in Victorville."

Craig replies, "Holy shit!!! …Do you think this was just a prank phone call? …Did Axel just get me to drive three hours round trip to fuck with me?"

Megan: "It's possible… It would be a pretty ingenious trick (she laughs)… He knows you have a hard-on for him. It's pretty easy to assume that you'd drive that far if he said he was going to kill someone there."

Craig: "And I bet Brooke helped him cook this one up… OK, I'm coming home. This type of threat is illegal, especially to a cop. I'll have to look up the violation code tomorrow. Axel AND Brooke will regret this shit."

Megan: "You may wanna let this one go, Craig. If the rest of the station finds out about this colossal prank you fell for, they'll never let you live it down. (laughs some more)"

Craig: "I'll think about that… In the meantime, call Victorville P.D. and put out an APB on Axel's car. Better to be safe than sorry in case it wasn't a prank."

Megan: "No problem."

Craig: "Megan, one more thing… I know it's late, but could you go by Brooke's apartment to check on her. If Axel did do something to her, there'll be evidence there, and if not, I'd like to know she's safe."

Megan: "I'll go right now and call you back in 15 minutes."

But the police had responded to Axel's 9-1-1 call and arrived at Brooke's apartment at 12:20am. By the time Megan arrives there at 12:50, the area is already taped off as a crime scene, and there are a dozen cops collecting evidence. Megan knows all the cops on the scene. She enters the apartment and sees Brooke with her head bashed in. She nearly vomits at the sight.

One of her jackass crime scene colleagues has a sampling device that plays back audio at the touch of a button. He approaches Megan and as cheesy as possible says, "Head bashed in, strangled and stabbed. Too bad she's not a cat. She'd have" (removes his glasses), "SIX… LIVES…LEFT."… "Yeaaaaaaaaaaaaaaaaaaaaah!" Roger Daulty of The Who screams from the audio device.

He cracks himself up, but Megan's not amused. She says, "Hey, Caruso, who's in charge of the investigation?" She's taken to Detective McDowell. She knows him; he's a big, intimidating looking black guy, but he's a genuinely friendly guy and a good cop. Megan asks what they've found so far. He tells her, "A 9-1-1 call came in at about 11:50pm. When the responding officers got here, the door was partly open and they found her like this.

89

So far they collected a bloody bat, and there's a knife still in the body. There's also marks around her neck, strangled, probably rope. We won't know which one was cause of death for a day or two."

Megan tells him, "Craig saw Axel Simmons here with Brooke earlier tonight. Shortly after, Axel called him and admitted to kidnapping her. Craig's been out searching for them."

Officer McDowell informs her, "Axel will be closely looked at, but we can't arrest him tonight based on Craig's word." Detective McDowell already knows about Brooke's call to the police against Craig, and he knows their history together.

He says, "Look, I know Craig is your partner, but it's just as likely that Craig may have done this and is trying to pin it on Axel. If any physical evidence places Axel in the apartment, he'll be picked up and arrested, I promise. But if we question him now with no real evidence, we can't hold him. And if he takes off, we may never find him. It'll take a day to get some results back from the lab. Just be a little patient."

Megan tells him, "I know Craig... You know Craig. He didn't kill her! I'm positive Axel did! When we arrested Axel with those weapons, we had to let him go... and we knew he'd do something like this! Don't let him get away again!... "

McDowell says, "You know I'll do my job. I like Craig and I don't think he did this, but we have to clear him. Have him see me tomorrow to give a statement."

As Megan is leaving, she hears that same jackass talking to someone in the background, "This girl liked heavy metal … And somebody BANGED… HER… HEAD..." "Yeaaaaaaaaaaaaaah!"

Megan calls Craig and informs him that Brooke is dead and tells him the whole situation. She adds, "Tomorrow they should have some results back. It's just a matter of time. The crime scene was a brutal mess. I'm sure he made a mistake and left something we can use."

Craig sees McDowell in the morning and tells him everything he knows. McDowell is giving Craig the benefit of the doubt and does not arrest him while he proceeds with the investigation. But a few hours later, fingerprints on the bat come back as a match to Craig. So around the time Axel is making friends with Jake the dog, Officer Craig Carter is arrested for murder.

A search warrant is issued to search Craig's vehicle and house. The search team notices the missing knife in the cutlery set and takes the rest of the set as evidence. They take samples from the red spots on the counter and wall and vent. They open the vent and find the rope, and the pictures, and the bloody fingerprints of four separate women!

When interrogated by Detective McDowell, Craig has no answers. Craig doesn't even believe they have this evidence he's told about. He thinks, 'it must be a lie - I know police tactics, they're lying to sweat me out. They're treating me like a common suspect to get a confession out of me. But I'm innocent. I know they can't have evidence that I'm a serial killer. That's absurd. All they have is the restraining order and my admission to being at Brooke's doorstep. Why can't they see it was Axel like I know it was Axel?... Maybe they're sweating him in another interrogation room?'

But with this much evidence against Craig, and not a trace of evidence physical against Axel, Detective McDowell never even questions Axel... Just as Axel planned!!!

It takes a couple days to hit the tv, but one day after Axel sees the Smiths on the news, he catches this:

"Today's top story: Police have a suspect in custody this evening they believe to be a serial killer here in LA. Three separate murders, previously believed to be unrelated to each other, and a new murder of a prostitute have been linked together by investigators. And what's worse is that the suspect is someone charged with protecting us! Police Officer Craig Carter of the LAPD was arrested yesterday. They're dubbing him 'The Fingerprint Killer' because he apparently took his victims fingerprints with their own blood and kept them as souvenirs … Scaaaary!…Ok Sammy, tell us about weather…"

Megan has been informed of all the new evidence. She can't make sense of it; she doesn't want to believe it. She thought she knew Craig so well, but she can't stop thinking… 'the evidence is indisputable!... Not only Brooke, but he killed three other women? Was Craig trying to use me as a possible alibi when he called, supposedly on his way to Victorville???... Oh my god…

92

a serial killer had been watching my back on the job for the last four years!!! Was he going to kill ME eventually?'

Megan has to confront him - she can't resist. She pulls some strings to get him in a room in lock-up to talk. Megan enters and Craig is still not convinced that the evidence he was told about is real.

Craig: "Megan... Do you believe they arrested ME? How could they really believe I killed Brooke?... Cops are supposed to stick together."

Megan: "They didn't tell you?"

Craig: "Tell me what?"

And Megan lists for him again ALL of the evidence that McDowell told him about.

Craig: "Wait, wait, wait... That's all real??? I thought they were working me over..."

Megan: "It's real... They've got you... Just tell me, Craig, HOW could you?... How could you kill four women? You were such a close friend... help me understand... why?" (she's misting up and almost has tears in her eyes).

Craig: "Wait... I did NOT do any of this!... You can't believe I did these murders. There has to be another explanation... Help me figure it out!"

Megan: "Come on!... How could you be innocent and there be this much concrete evidence???"

Craig: "Give me the benefit of the doubt just for a minute and help me figure out how this is happening... Axel is behind it somehow."

Megan: "You know, the case against you is so strong, he's not even a suspect anymore. It's only you in the crosshairs now."

Craig: "Well, let's try to explain the evidence piece by piece."

Megan (in a challenging tone): "Ok, at the crime scene, the bat that crushed Brooke's skull had your fingerprints on it, and the knife in her chest was from your kitchen."

Craig: "Ok, I can't explain that… for now..."

Megan: "Brooke was also strangled. There were marks on her neck, and a rope was found hidden in your house in a heating vent."

Craig: "OK, I have no idea how that got there... What else?"

Megan: "There was a page of Brooke's bloody fingerprints in the same vent! …Along with similar pages and pictures of three other dead women."

Craig: "Let's start with that. Who were the other women?"

Megan gives him a brief description of the other three girls and the description of those three crime scenes.

Craig: "These were planted. These were planted by Axel! They had to have been... Axel was in my house... He's a locksmith. He could've easily gotten into my house… And he took all those items, the knife, the bat…"

Megan: "You know that sounds crazy and desperate, right?"

Craig: "But it explains it all… There's no witnesses to any of this..." Craig realizes for himself, "That's why he sent me to Victorsville!!! He needed time in my house!"

Megan starts to see some credibility in what Craig is reasoning out.

Craig: "He was going back and forth between Brooke's apartment and my house all night, setting me up! ...And I fell for it!"

Megan is looking through her evidence report:

Megan: "Most of this stuff COULD possibly be planted, but the paper with Brooke's blood fingerprints on it also had your fingerprints on the paper. Axel couldn't have just planted that?"

Craig thinks for a few seconds:

Craig: "Are you sure that report is right?... ...Hold on, the night we arrested Axel, he had fingerprint paper in his trunk!!! I must have touched it then. My fingerprints are on there from when it was just blank paper – Axel took Brooke's prints on it later..."

Megan is starting to believe him.

Megan: "I thought it was weird that he had fingerprint paper with him, packed with knives and latex gloves... We have it logged in from his arrest. Awfully coincidental that he has blank fingerprint paper and then a serial killer appears who takes his victim's fingerprints...That should be enough to at least make him a suspect again."

Craig: "Clearly, Axel killed those other three women. You won't find one connection from those murders back to me other than those blood fingerprints that Axel planted... Megan, you're the

95

only one who believes me right now. You gotta get me out of here!"

The police union procures a great defense attorney to represent Craig. They want him to be fairly represented; and if he's guilty, they don't want to give him easy grounds for appeal for inadequate council in such a serious case.

The attorney is Artie Walker. Artie has gone through all of the evidence and is certain that Craig is guilty of all four murders. He has his first meeting with Craig at the jail. They have their introductions and they talk alone:

Craig: "I'm not guilty of these charges. Do you believe me?"

Artie: "ALL of my clients are innocent Craig, and that fact is irrelevant anyway. My job is to get the best possible result for my client, and I intend to do that for you."

Craig tells Artie everything he hypothesized with Megan about. It sounds like an elaboration of a mad man. Artie doesn't buy it and KNOWS a jury would never believe it.

Artie says, "Look, Craig, here's what we're dealing with... I can not say in court something I know to be a lie, so I'm going to tell you what I think might have happened, and you just listen...

Maybe those first three murders were committed by three separate killers? Other than the existence of the blood fingerprints, there's no other reason to believe these murders were committed by the same killer. You, being a police officer, had

96

access to the crime scenes before other cops showed up. Or, maybe you had other time alone with the bodies. You could simply have taken the blood fingerprints when no-one was looking... That's not murder!... Maybe evidence tampering? But that's not as severe a charge…

That leaves Brooke, which is not so easy to explain. I'll be honest, they have you for her murder. There's no way around it. But I can probably knock it down to second degree instead of first degree murder. It wasn't premeditated, maybe a crime of passion…you have history with her… maybe she provoked you somehow… Second degree with a sympathetic remorseful defendant could have you out of jail in as little as ten years…

Before you speak, and tell me things I can't unhear, think for a second. If they convict you for more than Brooke's murder, you will have high profile serial killer status. You'll never see the outside of a maximum security prison – you could get the death penalty. And you, being a former cop AND convicted serial killer, would be a target and a trophy for the other hardened prisoners. You're aware of what happens in maximum security prisons, aren't you? …If I can get second degree on only Brooke, I may be able to get you into a medium security facility where you'll be a little safer… and it'll be closer to 10 years, not life… and not the death penalty."

Craig is sitting with his head in his hands now. He's absorbed all of this and sees his life passing him by. He looks up at Artie and pleads, "But I'm innocent. Axel framed me..."

Artie explains, "Once again, that's irrelevant, we have to face facts, and I'm not the one you need to convince. There will be twelve jurors petrified of letting a serial killer go free. If they see all this evidence and only a choice between completely guilty and completely innocent, you can kiss your life goodbye... Think about it...

I'm going to go to the district attorney now and see if he'll even deal second degree murder for Brooke and evidence tampering for the other three girls. If not, I can still sell it to a jury later. I'll be back tomorrow..."

In the meantime, Megan goes to Detective McDowell with her, and Craig's, theory on how Axel framed Craig. But McDowell isn't swayed; he is already convinced Craig is the killer. And the coincidence of Axel possessing fingerprint paper is not enough to go to a judge to issue a search warrant. Megan gets a similar response from her captain. She goes directly to a judge she's acquainted with, but the judge doesn't see enough to grant a search warrant.

Megan is not a homicide detective. It's not her job, but on her off hours, she puts on her uniform and goes to Axel's home; nobody else is going to talk to him. Axel answers the door and steps out onto the porch so that Megan can't look inside.

Axel: "Ah, Officer TRIXIE, how can I help you today?"

Megan: (in a very formal tone) "Axel, where were you the evening of April 20? The night Brooke was killed."

Axel: "I'd have to think about that. I'll have my lawyer get back to you. Or, maybe I'll just exercise my right to remain silent."

Megan: "I know you killed her… I know you killed those three other girls… and framed Craig."

Axel: "Well, you're a cop. You probably should arrest me… if you KNOW it."

Megan: "We figured out you had blank fingerprint paper in your car when we arrested you. That was clever to use that exact paper for Brooke. You pulled off a great set-up... And sending Craig to Victorsville… Very resourceful."

Axel: "I don't have any idea what you are talking about… Sounds like an exciting plan though. But Craig killed those poor girls... I never liked Craig. He seemed a little off, and he was a bully. … But hypothetically, if Craig isn't the real serial killer, you may want to TELL him: It looks like the killer really didn't NEED a patsy to take the fall. It seems this killer was getting away with his murders… But SOMEBODY got in his way… …hypothetically."

Megan: "This isn't over." She walks away.

Axel: "Bye Bye, TRIXIE."

Megan gets in her car and drives away. She knows, it may be over, though. She's at a dead end, and there's not much else she can do.

Artie visits Craig in jail the next day and explains the district attorney won't even consider pleading down to one count of second degree murder. Since it's made the news, and because there's so much evidence, there won't be any deal that will allow him to ever be free again... and it looks like they'll be pushing for the death penalty.

But Artie explains, "I should still be able to get a jury to see it as a single case of second degree murder at trial... if you take responsibility for Brooke's murder... and take the stand to explain how you only fingerprinted the other three girls... AFTER you found them already dead by someone else."

Craig: "Absolutely not! I've thought about it, and I can't say I'm guilty of anything I didn't do. I will take the stand and explain how Axel framed me. Megan believes in me, she'll testify. She's a cop, that'll help."

Artie: "She's a cop, but she's your partner and your friend. She has motive to lie on your behalf. The prosecution will tear her up on cross examination. We don't have enough facts to create reasonable doubt here."

Craig: "This can't really be happening... Is there any other way?"

Artie: "The only other defense I see that doesn't land you in a maximum security prison for the rest of your life, or on death row, is if you want me to go to the D.A. and say we'll be using an insanity defense. He might agree to sign off on 'not guilty by reason of insanity' if we offered to commit you to an asylum for the rest of your life. But I wouldn't recommend that."

Craig: "…I see no choice but to still try to convince a jury of the truth, that I'm innocent… Prepare the defense that Axel framed me."

Artie: "OK, this is your life and your call. I will do my best, but I don't think this will end well for you. We go to court tomorrow for your arraignment. We'll enter your plea of 'not guilty'. There is no chance of bail, but I'll put a motion in for it as a formality. I can push for a speedy trial. I usually recommend this to my clients that have a shot of walking after the trial, but I can drag this out if you want."

Craig: "I WILL be walking after the trial. Please get it scheduled as soon as possible."

At the arraignment, bail is denied - trial is scheduled to begin in one week.

But Craig isn't holding up so well under this immense pressure. Other than Megan, nobody he knows believes he's innocent. His other cop friends have completely turned their backs on him.

Craig doesn't have much family, but he's very close with his father, George Carter. George's wife (Craig's mother), died five years ago from breast cancer. George, heartbroken, never tried to meet anyone else. Since then, typically, Craig and his father would spend time together about twice a week. George is a retired military man; he spent most of his life in the service. He's a well respected, disciplined man with a lot of pride… George has not come to visit his son once, and has not taken his phone calls. This deeply hurts Craig… even his father thinks he's guilty.

Chapter 7

Vicky Takes Over

Axel behaves himself for a few days after Megan's visit. He doesn't like the fact that he so brilliantly disposed of one nosey cop only to replace him with another one. He's still considering moving out of the area soon.

Axel goes to work regularly and still gets the occasional dizzy spell and sharp head pain. Once in a while now, they're accompanied by a random phantom smell. Anything from vanilla candles to burnt cinnamon rolls to a distinct perfume his first girlfriend wore when he was sixteen. They feel like flashes of a distant memory, and then... gone.

A little more time goes by. Craig's upcoming trial is all over the news: 'The Fingerprint Killer trial' is set to begin in two days.

At Axel's work, a call comes in from a stranded woman (Dana) who locked her keys in her car. Axel's coworker offers an old tired joke, "Did you hear the one about the blonde who locked her keys OUT of her car?"

Axel is dispatched in the company van. As Axel spots Dana's car up the road in the distance (about 100 yards away), she's laying down on the front of the car – legs on the hood and back against the windshield. She's wearing a tight shirt and even from this distance, he can tell she is stacked and sexy... and blonde. Vicky immediately appears in Axel's passenger seat and takes an interest:

Vicky: "She's pretty Axel, isn't she?"

Axel: "NO!"

Vicky: "No, she's not pretty???"

Axel: "Yes, she IS pretty. But NO to what you are thinking. No more killing customers... especially with Officer Trixie on my ass."

Vicky: "But the Smiths were a successful murder/suicide. The cops didn't investigate. Your name and the locksmith company never appeared in the cop's report. It's like it never happened for us - it's a do-over. We still get one customer to kill."

Axel: "That's brilliant... But listen close... ...NO!!!!!!!!!!!!!!

...We don't want to draw ANY suspicion to ourselves that even may slightly impact on Craig's trial. He'll still be accusing me of the four murders. He'll look desperate because he only has the coincidence over my fingerprint paper. But if they can also say a customer on mine is recently missing or found dead, it'll lend some credibility to Craig's claims... So just be patient."

Axel greets Dana, and as standard procedure, copies her info off her driver's license for the work order - can't just unlock a car door for a stranger without verifying who they are. In no time, the job is done and everyone is on their way.

Vicky pouts over this lost opportunity the rest of the day. Axel ignores her and goes to bed about an hour earlier than normal. He wakes up in the morning and Vicky has made breakfast. She apologizes for being bitchy the previous day. Vicky seems to be in an especially perky mood. Her personality is generally upbeat and peppy, but today she seems extra-happy. Vicky tells Axel she has a present for him and gives him a gift-wrapped box – about the size a sweater would be wrapped in. She anxiously waits for him to open it, like a little girl giving her father what she thinks is the greatest present ever on Christmas Eve, because she can't wait until the morning for him to open it. Axel opens it and can't believe his eyes. It is the most terrifying thing he's ever seen... and he's seen a lot of terrifying things.

In the box is about $200 cash... a sheet of bloody fingerprints... and two pictures of Dana, one seemingly alive, and one definitely dead.

Axel is enraged:

Axel: "Vicky, what have you done?!!!!! ... Explain this!"

Vicky: "Calm down Axel. You would've been so proud of me. I learned my lessons well from the master. It was a perfect night - beautiful and meticulous."

Axel: "Tell me every detail and do NOT gloss over anything."

Vicky: "We had Dana's address from her driver's license. I packed one of your special bags and I drove over there and parked... a block away. I snuck around the back of her house. It was a one story house, so I was able to listen at every window. I could hear inside and I could tell the only people home were her and a guy. They were fucking. I was getting turned on just from listening from outside and picturing Dana getting nailed.

…So, I put on latex gloves and picked the lock on the back door. It was an easy one, I've watched you do these many times. I entered their bedroom with your gun drawn. They were doing it doggie-style facing the other way, so they didn't even realize I was in the room... By the way, watching doggie style from behind the guy is not the most flattering angle to watch sex...

I quietly approached them and cocked the gun next to his head, 'shick shick' and said 'FREEZE!' They just froze in mid-fuck, didn't make a peep. I said 'Do as I say and I won't have to kill you.' They were both very cooperative. They seemed like a nice couple. Too bad they did die so young… Anyhoo…

The husband's name was Gerald – good looking guy, muscular… I knew I couldn't put the gun down while I tied up Gerald because I would've been left vulnerable. So I made him handcuff his own hands together under the chair. Keep in mind, he's totally naked from just being interrupted having sex. I think he lost his boner before the gun made the second 'shick' noise though.

I made Dana handcuff her wrist to the opposite side of the bed so she couldn't pull any surprises while I dealt with Gerald. Then, I fully restrained Gerald to the chair with rope; he couldn't move his arms or legs at all. I'm a girl… I'm not taking any chances of being manhandled by a guy. And I sealed his mouth with duct tape.

Next, I turned my attention to the lovely Dana. I kept the gun pointed at her and unlocked her handcuffs, so she was unrestrained. Dana wasn't completely naked. She had some lingerie on that was pulled up while they were fucking. I pulled over a chair, and sat, and told her to do a striptease for me. She took off the lingerie, but I was very disappointed in the effort she showed in teasing as she stripped... but what a gorgeous body. She must work out a lot. And those huge boobs of hers... they're real!

...Now that she's completely naked, I get her cuffed to all four corners of the bed and tape her mouth. I grope her, and taste her, and have some fun with her... I looked over, and Gerald's got his boner back. He liked watching me pleasure his wife... What a sick freak!

...About now, I realized, I had a penis, so I..."

Axel stops her mid-sentence, "Woe, hang on there! ...Did you just say you had a penis?"

Vicky replies casually, "Yes, I had a penis... OK... I had YOUR penis."

Axel is stunned, "My penis??? What the hell does that mean?" He reaches in his pants to check himself.

Vicky tells him, "Well, silly, I don't have a real body... so... I had to BORROW yours. You were sleeping; you weren't using it, so I just borrowed it for a little bit."

Axel is dumbfounded. He was standing, but sits immediately, thinking of the potential ramifications of what he's hearing. After a minute he tells Vicky to continue with the story.

Vicky continues, "...So I realized I have a penis, and I know it's your penis, and I want to take care of YOUR penis... so, I put on a condom ... YOU'RE WELCOME!

...I put on the condom and start fucking Dana... Oh... My... God! What a great feeling. I'm already super-excited just be WITH her, but to actually be inside her while fucking her. I can't describe it... Well, you know, you've done it before... Actually, you've done it to me... so again, YOUR WELCOME!...

...And it's a feeling of power. I never thought I had penis envy before, but now ... I totally have penis envy ... I want a penis, there, I said it...

Anyway, looking at her tits bounce as I repeatedly thrust inside her and looking into her crying eyes, I'm so excited that I cum within, like, a minute. I have no idea how you last so long. Maybe I just need some more practice... So I get up and flush the condom...three times. See, I'm always thinking.

I was still turned on though; I never lost the erection, so I put on another condom. But I feel like I want something a little different. So I did something a little risky... Don't get mad..."

Axel is starting to scowl so Vicky goes in a different direction.

Vicky says, "...I fucked Gerald in the ass..."

Vicky pauses for a couple seconds and then can't hold in the laugh. She continues, "… Axel, the look on your face is priceless. I'm fucking with you. No, I never touched Gerald.

The different thing I was GOING to say was… I just wanted to feel Dana's arms around me while I fucked her. It's a girl thing, more intimate. I'm sure you wouldn't relate. I know I couldn't risk freeing both of her arms, so I just unlocked her right wrist. I told her to close her eyes and pretend I was Gerald. I wanted her to give me the Dana experience more than I was getting with her unable to move.

It was better… but… well… sorry about the scratches on your back... She's a wildcat that one. I don't think she was trying to hurt me - she was still pretty scared – they're just sex scratches."

Axel becomes increasingly alarmed. He goes to the bathroom mirror and checks his back to see if it was really true… There ARE scratches on his back! He chastises Vicky, "Do you know what this means?!!! My skin cells are now under Dana's fingernails!"

Vicky replies, "Don't worry, I took care of it. I'll get to that soon.

…Anyway, I blew my second load… I love saying that now, so manly… I used to hate to hear guys talk crude like that… I blew my second load and flushed the condom… three times.

Then for some reason I got really sleepy... What's with that? ...And I had no desire to play with Dana anymore.

So I took Dana's 'before' picture and I re-cuffed her free arm to the bedpost.

I really didn't FEEL quite like even slicing up her face with the surgical scalpel,
or seeing if I could rip her nipples off with the needle nose pliers, or heating the extra large hunting knife blade with the blowtorch until it was glowing red and ramming it up her cunt...
...But I did it all... and it was fun again once I started... Just needed that extra adrenaline boost.

But I wanted more toys; your selection was boring me... In their garage, I found a circular saw... but I thought that might be too loud for nighttime. Then I found a drill. I tested it. It was pretty quiet - and they had a pretty long drill bit already installed. I plugged it in to the bedroom wall and drilled into Dana's arms and legs probably 40 or 50 times. She couldn't talk because of the duct tape, but I'm pretty sure she was pretty mad at me by now. I finished her by drilling through her chest slowly into her heart... ...Then she was dead. I took her picture and her fingerprints... And I wiped her fingers clean with toilet paper that I then flushed three times.

Gerald was not having a good time any more either, his dick was limp again. I drilled through his penis and into the chair. Then I drilled through the back of his head into his brain... All dead..."

Vicky pauses as if she's done with the story. Axel inquires impatiently, "How exactly does this play out as a murder/suicide?"

Vicky responds, "It's not... What I left out of the beginning of the story is that as I was driving to their neighborhood, I noticed a lot of tagging by gangs. I saw one symbol about ten times. It wasn't a very complicated scribble, in red letters, so I got an idea. I made a detour to a home improvement store that was open 'til midnight and I bought some red spray-paint. Fast forward to the end of the night - I sprayed that symbol on two walls in Dana and Gerald's bedroom and again on their living room wall... And then I carved the symbol, with the surgical scalpel, onto Dana's dead belly... and again on Gerald's dead forehead...

They must have done something awful to piss off the neighborhood gang.

Then it's just pack up and take some cash."

Axel is impressed, but he's not satisfied, "What about my skin cells under her fingernails?"

Vicky points to the freezer in the kitchen. Axel opens the freezer and sees five finger end digits in a baggie.

Vicky says, "I even thought enough to not take her whole hand. Those fingertips should be easy enough to get rid of. You can clean the fingernails to your satisfaction and just flush them down a public toilet somewhere. Or keep them to plant on somebody... maybe Officer Trixie?"

Axel has to admit, "Vicky, it sounds like you did think of everything. I'm pleasantly surprised... And I'm even more in awe of how truly deranged and twisted you are." He stands and approaches her and gives her a little kiss on the lips, "... But don't ever... EVER, borrow my body again!"

Axel sits down and takes a bite of his breakfast Vicky had prepared for him. Vicky's glowing from the high praise. She responds to the other issue, "But I thought you liked when I made you breakfast... or dinner after a nap?"

Axel's mind reverberates, 'Holly shit, she's been using my body whenever I sleep! What else might she be up to?' It's an extremely sobering thought.

Chapter 8

The Trial Begins / Introducing Danielle

The trial of Officer Craig Carter, 'The Fingerprint Killer', starts today. The phrase 'media circus' doesn't even begin to describe the amount of coverage this trial has attracted. It's the leading story on every news program, every night, across the country. There are experts giving opinions on every miniscule detail. If Craig's lawyer takes his dog to the vet and there is video, it's considered 'breaking news', and these experts are discussing the ramifications a sick pet could have on his concentration level in the courtroom. There are 24-hour news stations dedicating virtually all 24 hours to this trial. There are surveys from every channel, and based on just the details released to the public over the last week, over 90 percent of the population thinks Craig is guilty of all four murders. One station tracked down O.J. for comment: "Oh yea, no doubt. That white boy's gettin' da lethal injection."

Craig still hasn't heard from his father, but a few times on TV, he sees "reporters" staking out his father's house and asking horrifying questions as he walks by: "Mr. Carter, do you think your son killed those four girls?" "George Carter, are you afraid of your son?" "George, do you think there was anything you could've done raising Craig that could have prevented him from becoming a serial killer?"

George never answers their questions or even acknowledges their presence; he just walks by. But one time, the questioning brought him to tears as he was walking back to his house. Craig caught this on TV. Seeing his father crying, thinking his son was a serial killer, brought Craig to tears himself.

After Vicky's indiscretion with his body, Axel convinces Vicky that it's best to not murder anyone until after the verdict is handed down. Vicky is actually on board this time.

Axel is anxiously looking forward to watching the trial on TV. To see his plan presented piece by piece to the world is very exciting. That the trial is televised is going to be a good distraction from killing for Axel.

But as much as Axel would love to sit home all day and watch trial coverage, he has to go to work. He sets his DVR to record all day, and he'll watch at night. The day goes smoothly with most customers giving their unsolicited take on Craig's guilt; it's a great small-talk news item.

Axel's co-worker, Freddy, invites Axel to join him at a sports bar after work to watch the ball game on TV. He claims they have the best burgers around. Axel will need to eat dinner, and he knows Vicky won't be cooking for him (he wasn't planning a nap), so he agrees to go – but only long enough to eat. He's not staying for the whole game; he has opening statements to watch.

They get to the bar, get a table, and order a couple burgers and a couple beers. It turns out, these ARE great burgers.

Freddy rambles on (he's not an intellectual), "I was thinking about this earlier today... How do you think the field of gynecology got started? I mean one day there's no gynecologists, and the next day some dude opens a shop and says – Lay back, and throw your legs in the air... I'm gonna look into your vagina... just to make sure everything's alright... Oh, and in addition, you pay me!!!... You pay me the equivalent of a hundred dollars – probably a bunch of chickens or yams or something. Does that not sound like a scam. What woman falls for that? I think it was definitely a scam, it just became legit after a while..."

About half way through their meal, Freddy's cell phone rings. Axel deduces from his half of the conversation that it's an ex-girlfriend - this is a booty call. Freddy apologizes for bailing, "I didn't know she was coming to town, and she'll be gone tomorrow."

Axel completely understands. He stays by himself to finish his meal.

After Freddy's gone, Vicky strolls in and sits with Axel as he finishes the burger. They chat for a couple minutes while Axel finishes his beer. Vicky notices, "Hey Axel, that woman sitting at the bar is checking us out."

Axel looks over. There IS a woman by herself glancing over in his direction. She has brown hair, about shoulder length. She's mid-thirties, relatively close to Axel's age. She's cute, but kind of soccer-mom wholesome looking - not the type to be looking

115

at a COUPLE in a bar. Or can she not see Vicky at all? …Axel can't tell.

Vicky's staring down the mystery woman as seductively as she can. Axel tells her, "Don't stare so blatantly. Glance away a little, you'll scare her."

Vicky says without looking away from the woman, "I know what I'm doing. Women can stare. It's not so intimidating. If YOU were to stare like this, you'd come off like … like a serial killer."

Vicky summons the woman over with a motion of her head, and she comes to their table and introduces herself, "Hi, I'm Danielle."

They invite her to sit, and they talk; they all hit it off right away. Danielle touches both Axel's and Vicky's arms and shoulders, gesturing while she talks - clear body language that she's interested… in both of them. After about 30 minutes Danielle has to go, but they exchange phone numbers.

Once she's gone, Vicky casually notes, "She's not my usual type… but I like her."

Axel says firmly but quietly, "Do NOT kill her!"

Vicky assures him she won't kill Danielle. Axel looks at the paper, and her phone number is 555-6969. He realizes, it's bogus. The 555 prefix is only for fake phone numbers; why would she do that?

Axel and Vicky go home to watch the trial.

Opening statements:

Representing the people, Kyle Branson:

"Ladies and gentlemen of the jury… this is a very serious case. Four women have been murdered by a man not motivated by fear or greed or anger or revenge or jealousy or any human emotion I could explain or that you could relate to. They were murdered to satisfy lust, lust for blood… He did it for fun! He raped and tortured and mutilated these four girls extensively, and he must be stopped. YOU must stop him in this courtroom. Do not set him free.

I am about to show you crime scene pictures of what Craig Carter did to these four girls. They will be difficult to look at, but you must know what kind of animal we're dealing with:"

(crime scene picture #1 is displayed by computer slide show on a white screen). "Stephanie was found with virtually every bone in her body broken. She was beaten relentlessly with a metal pipe. Her face was beaten so badly, her parents couldn't recognize pictures of her. It took DNA matching to the parents to verify it was Stephanie... Here's an earlier picture of her. She was a very pretty girl..."

(crime scene picture #2 is displayed). "Wendy was found with her chest cut open, ribs broken out, and her heart badly damaged. She was still alive when the killer ripped out bones, reached into her chest and squeezed her heart until she died..."

(crime scene picture #3 is displayed). "Jessica was mutilated with a paring knife. There were ELEVEN stab wounds on her body and a deep cut on her left arm that went from her wrist all the way up to her shoulder. She bled to death…. She was two months pregnant..."

(Axel comments to Vicky, "Actually, they got that one wrong. Cause of death was suffocation.")

(crime scene picture #4 is displayed). "And finally Brooke: Her head was brutally bashed in with a baseball bat. She was also strangled with a rope. Coroners couldn't conclusively determine which caused her death... But after she was dead, still not satisfied, Craig drove a steak knife into her heart…"

Kyle continues, "That Craig Carter was a trusted police officer at the time he committed these murders makes these heinous crimes even more egregious. These were brutal murders, and if this man goes free (points to Craig), there WILL be more victims. It could be your daughter, or someone you're close to next time."

For the defense, Artie Walker stands:

"This is a high profile case, and I know all of you have seen some stuff on the TV, and you may have opinions already. But in a court of law, you're directed to put aside any preconceived notions of guilt the media may have conveyed. Their objective is to get ratings, and calling a police officer a serial killer gets ratings. I ask you to keep an open mind when weighing the evidence. If you do, you'll see there's another alternative...

The prosecution is showing you these pictures to scare and outrage you, and you should be scared and outraged. But your job isn't to determine IF something horrible has been done. Your job is to determine WHO did these horrible things. Don't let your emotions lead you to convict an innocent man."

The prosecution will call its first witness tomorrow.

The next day starts with no surprises for Axel; he goes to work, gets a couple dizzy spells, and goes home to watch more of the trial from today's DVR recording. Shortly after he starts watching, there's a knock at the door. Axel stands up, but Vicky answers the door first... It is Danielle??? Axel naturally looks surprised... because he is surprised. He asks, "How did ya know where I live?"

Danielle replies, "Vicky invited me to come over and watch the trial with you guys... I brought a pie." She puts the pie on the kitchen table.

Axel asks, "Why did you give me a fake phone number? I thought you didn't want to see us again."

She replies, "It wasn't a fake number. Do you still have it? ...Call it."

Axel easily remembers the number: 555-6969. He dials it on his cell phone, but he's sure it won't work...

...There's a ring that comes from Danielle's purse. She takes out the phone and answers, "Hello Axel..." Axel ponders, 'So it WAS her real number... Weird.'

Vicky breaks out a bottle of wine. They talk and eat Danielle's pie (get your mind out of the gutter). And they watch the prosecution present its case:

Kyle calls a witness to authenticate the recording Brooke made of Craig blackmailing her for sex (from her pen gadget). Then he calls a witness that corroborate that Brooke obtained a restraining order against Craig. Kyle's next witness authenticates Brooke's call to the police, the evening of her murder, to complain that Craig broke that restraining order. It places Craig at the scene of the murder and adds to motive. The defense does nothing here - no cross examinations.

The prosecution calls their forensic scientist to the stand. He explains the bat found in Brooke's apartment had Brooke's blood all over it, and it also had Craig's fingerprints on it. He testifies that the knife found in Brooke's body matched a knife missing from Craig's kitchen knife set. He details that the rope found hidden in Craig's heating vent had Brooke's skin cells on it, and that the strangulation marks on Brooke's neck is consistent with this type of rope.

In cross examination, the defense asks if it's POSSIBLE that somebody took Craig's bat from his house, killed Brooke with it and left it behind. The expert has to admit "It's possible." Similar questioning followed about the knife and the rope. Again, the expert has to admit, "It's possible," but it's obvious to everybody in the courtroom the likelihood is very slim.

The trial is moving quickly because all Artie can do is try to coax the words 'it's possible' out of each witness. It really doesn't make a strong case for the defense, but it is hard to defend Craig against the mountain of evidence against him.

Court is adjourned for the day...

Axel turns off the TV. He has many more hours recorded of expert analysis, essentially journalistic masturbation, but he knows it's going well for the team he's rooting for without the expert's help.

Danielle isn't ready to leave. She's a little tipsy from the wine (a second and third bottle came out as the trial went on, so they're all a little tipsy). Danielle scoots a little closer to Vicky, and they're looking deep into each other's eyes. Axel's noticed what's going on, and the room is silent. Everyone senses what's coming, but they're all afraid to make the first move. Then, Vicky steps up and leans in for a kiss. Danielle kisses back, and it's a deep passionate French kiss.

Axel's not sure his place in all of this, so he just waits patiently to see if he'll be invited to join in. The girls grope each other, and their tops come off. They do invite Axel to participate, and they all go into the bedroom.

In a new three-way like this, a main concern is that two of the people will be more into each other, and the third person doesn't get enough attention. That's not the case here! Danielle started with Vicky, but she wants them both equally.

They end up in multiple positions, as you might imagine. But it's always Danielle in the middle; meaning, Axel never penetrates Vicky...

Vicky eats out Danielle while Danielle blows Axel, Axel fucks Danielle while Danielle eats out Vicky...

They end up in a configuration where Vicky is lying on the bed face up. Danielle is licking her clit and fucking her with two fingers. Danielle is standing with her legs straight and far apart making a wide upside down V; and she's bent over at the hips at about 90 degrees to get her fingers and face to Vicky's pussy. Danielle is completely bent over with legs spread wide for Axel. Axel first kneels and takes a taste of her pussy, and then he gets up and fucks her from behind.

They all relish in this position for a little while, and Vicky is the first to start climaxing. As she builds, Danielle starts to cum also. They're in sync as they both hit the very peak of their orgasms. They're squirming, and gyrating, and moaning, and are completely overwhelmed in the moment, when something very unexpected happens... unexpected to Axel at least. He cums too. Axel never cums without death, or at least extreme violence. But tonight, all three of them have a simultaneous orgasm.

When it's all over and they're all exhausted, they pile on the bed. Axel is in the middle, and both girls rest their heads on his chest. Good times!... But Axel has a feeling this is going to get complicated... very soon.

The next day after work, Vicky approaches Axel. He can feel a talk coming up. But Vicky is totally cool with everything. She explains that as long as she gets the attention she needs from Axel, and they find new victims after the trial, they can keep fucking Danielle.

But what soon happens is Danielle is getting a little more of Axel's attention than Vicky. Danielle is a new toy, and she actually made Axel cum. Vicky helped too, but he was inside Danielle when it happened, so he wants to explore this a little more.

They have sex as a threesome the next night and all is still good. But the following night, Axel takes a drive with only Danielle to the beach. They light a bonfire and end up skinny dipping in the ocean. It's fuckin' cold, but they don't care - it adds to the excitement. Axel fucks Danielle as they stand chest deep in the cold dark ocean. He's able to cum inside her again.

What they don't see is Vicky, off in the distance, on the beach. She's staring at them, getting jealous, getting mad...

Nothing is ever spoken between Axel and Vicky about this encounter.

The trial is proceeding and Axel watches his recordings daily: Kyle introduces more witnesses and presents more evidence.

The traces of Brooke's blood in Craig's apartment: The prosecution proves it was there. The defense can only get the small concession that it's 'possible' it could have been planted.

The pictures and blood fingerprints of the dead girls: Kyle calls a scientist to testify that they are authentic and police witnesses to testify that they were found in Craig's heating vent. The defense can get the police witness to say 'it's possible' they were planted. But this witness gets frustrated, and is tired of being bullied, and adds, "It's POSSIBLE your mother killed all these girls… it doesn't make it at all realistic."

That statement stung Artie and Craig a little, but the jury was already thinking it.

Now Kyle focuses in on what he considers his strongest piece of evidence. He has the forensic scientist back on the stand to explain:

Kyle: "Doctor, please explain what exhibit 25-D is."

Doctor: "This red pattern is Brooke's blood. The blood was on her fingers, and then her fingers were methodically pressed to this paper. It's Brooke's fingerprints taken in her own blood."

Kyle: "Is there anything else on this paper the court should know about?"

Doctor: "Yes. We lifted other fingerprints that are not visible to the naked eye from the paper... They are a match to Craig Carter."

It took several days to enter all of the physical evidence and have experts authenticate it.

The prosecution calls Detective Martin McDowell to bring it all home:

Kyle: "Officer, you were in charge of the investigation of Brooke Jensen's murder?"

McDowell: "That is correct."

Kyle: "You are aware of all of the evidence of the case?"

McDowell: "I am thoroughly aware of every aspect of this case."

Kyle: "What do you believe happened?"

McDowell: "Without a doubt, Craig Carter killed all four women. There's an abundance of evidence both at the crime scene and at his home to prove he killed Brooke. And the blood fingerprints we found of the other three girls make it clear that he killed them also."

Prosecution is done with this witness. Artie stands for the defense.

Artie: "Why do you think there's virtually no evidence at the first three crime scenes and so much evidence that incriminates Craig at Brooke's apartment?"

McDowell: "I can't really say for sure... I could guess that he ran out of time, or maybe murdering Brooke was more personal to him. He had a turbulent history with her. Maybe he just snapped after this murder and didn't clean up... Maybe he wanted to get caught this time."

Artie: "But at least you admit, the crime scene at Brooke's is very different in this way than the other three crime scenes?"

McDowell: "Yes, it's different."

Artie: "And to clarify one more time, only Brooke's crime scene had ANY evidence that points to Craig Carter?"

McDowell: "Yes."

Artie: "Last question. Did you ever investigate Axel Simmons as a suspect in Brooke's murder?"

McDowell: "We considered him based on Craig's early statements, but as lab results came in, they all proved Craig was the killer. No physical evidence implicated Axel at all, so Craig's statements were deemed self-serving lies."

Artie: "So you never even investigated Axel Simmons?"

McDowell: "That's correct... There're also millions of other people in this city we didn't investigate for this murder... because there was no reason to."

(Axel does not like the accusation in this highly televised trial).

The defense is done with this witness... And the prosecution rests. It's a very strong case.

Later that evening Craig's informed that his father is dead. He was found when a reporter heard a gunshot go off in his house. George Carter was found in his military uniform with a self-inflicted gunshot wound to the temple of his head.

Craig cried for hours. He knows it's somewhat his fault. His father killed himself over the shame that his son is a serial killer…

'But I'm not a serial killer… Axel framed me!'

Meanwhile, the evening after the skinny-dipping, Danielle comes over again to visit Vicky and Axel. Axel's on the couch intently watching his recording of the day's trial, and Vicky is in the kitchen. Danielle sits in a kitchen chair to be near Vicky. Danielle has no idea how upset Vicky is about her and Axel having sex without her. Danielle is facing out towards the living room where Axel is, and she's looking at the TV from the distance. Vicky casually walks to the knife block on the counter, pulls out the large chef's knife, and casually approaches Danielle from behind. Vicky wraps her left arm around Danielle's forehead to secure her head against her waist and brings the blade to Danielle's throat with her right hand. Danielle's head is restrained, and she can't move with the knife at her throat.

Vicky calls out to Axel, "Axel… You like this cunt more than me?"

Axel turns and tries to calm her down from across the room, "Hey… Hang on there Vicky. You're my number one girl. You know that. Danielle's just a plaything for both of us... I thought you liked her too?"

Vicky replies, "I did like her... until you started screwing her behind my back..." (she recalls a position they all had sex in) "I mean without me knowing... You shouldn't be keeping secrets from me Axel!"

Axel responds, "I wasn't keeping secrets. We went for a drive, and it led to sex. I would've told you. I didn't think you'd care... Just let her go... You agreed, no more killing 'til after the trial... And absolutely not in our house."

Vicky says morbidly, "Perfect!" and slices Danielle's throat. The blood streams out of the wound and Danielle drops to the floor in a pool of her own blood. Axel is stunned.

Vicky is hysterical, out of her mind, "You made me do that! I had to do it... for you... You left me no choice! ...You just admitted to killing people... with her in the room. You said 'no more killing until after the trial'. She would have gone to the police... and Craig would have his reasonable doubt."

Vicky starts crying uncontrollably and muttering, "I did it for you... ... I did it for you ... ... I did it for you."

Axel is overwhelmed by all of this and takes Vicky in his arms to comfort her. He pacifies her, "It's all right... Everything's gonna be fine... We're gonna be just fine..." She's crying into his shoulder.

After a few minutes, Vicky starts to pull herself together. Axel is still holding Vicky in his arms with his back is to Danielle's dead body, and Vicky is facing her. Axel says in a calm voice, "We have to think about what to do with her body."

Vicky pulls back from Axel's arms just a little so she can see his face and says with an eerie calmness, "Axel... I already took care of it." She sniffles and wipes some tears from her face with her right hand.

Axel turns towards Danielle and starts to say, "What do you mean you took care ..." And he can't believe his eyes. In the spot that Danielle was just lying, dead, was no Danielle. There was still her pool of blood though.

Axel thinks, 'She was dead, right?... She couldn't have walked away?' And as he asks these questions to himself and stares down at the pool of blood, it starts to vanish until there's no trace that Danielle was ever there.

Axel looks to Vicky with a puzzled look. She just shrugs her shoulders as if to say 'I don't know.' But he's sure she knows something.

The defense begins their case and calls to the stand Officer Megan White. Megan approaches the stand wearing her police uniform.

Artie: "In your job as a police officer, you sometimes disguise yourself as a prostitute to catch men who frequent prostitutes?"

Megan: "That's correct."

Artie: "Did you ever arrest Axel Simmons?"

Megan: "Yes, myself and Officer Craig Carter arrested Axel when he tried to solicit me for sex. He said he wanted anal sex and to tie me up and smack me around… He gave me the creeps."

Artie: "Did you search Axel Simmons' car that evening."

Megan: "Yes, we did a routine search and found a number of disturbing items."

Artie has pictures he hands to Megan. During Axel's incarceration, these pictures were taken when the items were processed.

Artie: "Please identify if you found these items in Axel's car that evening and state what the items are for the record."

Megan: "All of these items were from his car. There's a big hunting knife, a smaller hunting knife, a utility knife, a large kitchen knife, a scalpel, a blindfold, four pairs of latex gloves, a blowtorch, needle nose pliers, acid, four pairs of handcuffs, duct tape, several lengths of rope, two garbage bags, rags, a change of clothes, a Polaroid camera, and fingerprint paper, like the kind police use."

Artie hands the photos to the jury.

Artie: "What did you think when you found these items?"

Kyle stands up, "I object. Her thoughts on the items are not relevant to the facts of the case."

Artie: "Your honor, I'm asking her professional opinion as a trained police officer."

Judge: "I'll allow it."

Megan: "These items, taken individually, could be completely innocent. But put them all together in a bag, and you have a kit to murder and torture. I thought Axel was a murderer. But we didn't have enough evidence to prosecute him."

Artie: "You mentioned you and Craig found fingerprint paper... anything significant about that?"

Megan: "Well, at first, it was a routine search, so Craig searched the vehicle with bare hands. He didn't wear latex gloves at first. That's how his fingerprints got on that fingerprint paper. Axel later used this same paper to take Brooke's prints in her blood and plant that paper in Craig's house."

Artie: "Do you believe Craig Carter is guilty of these four murders?"

Megan: "I am positive he is not! Axel Simmons killed them and framed Craig."

Artie: "Why do you believe this?"

Megan: "On the night Brooke was murdered, Craig called me and said he spotted Axel picking Brooke up on Sunset Boulevard. Craig went to her apartment and tried to warn Brooke that Axel was dangerous. Later that evening Axel called Craig and said he kidnapped Brooke and told Craig to come meet them in Victorville. I was on the phone to Craig as he was driving out there to SAVE Brooke. It was all a ruse to get Craig out of the city so Axel could get into his house, plant evidence, and take Craig's bat and steak knife to plant at the crime scene."

Artie: "As a police officer, are there any other facts about this case that don't seem quite right to you?"

Megan: "Yes. The first three girls were murdered by a very careful person. He left no trace that would lead back to himself... The Brooke Jensen crime scene was littered with evidence... all against Craig. Either the same person didn't commit all four murders, or more likely, they carefully and intentionally planted evidence at the last crime scene to incriminate Craig."

Artie: "What do you think of Officer McDowell's conclusions in this case?"

Megan: "I understand his position, but he's wrong. There's a lot of evidence against Craig, but everything can be explained away."

Artie: "You were Craig's partner and friend, and we've heard some pretty horrible stuff about him: accused of murders, blackmailing a prostitute for sex. Tell us about the man."

Megan: "Craig is a good man, a good cop. He isn't perfect. He shouldn't have treated Brooke the way he did. But I know he didn't kill her. He didn't kill any of those girls. He's not a serial killer. No matter how bad it looks, he didn't do it. Axel set him up."

The defense is finished with this witness. Kyle rises for the prosecution's cross examination:

Kyle: "Ms. White, you said you were talking to Craig on the phone as he drove out to Victorville. What time did he first call you that evening?"

Megan: "It was about 11:15 pm."

Kyle: "Are you aware of Brooke's time of death?"

Megan: "The coroner placed it between 9:00 and 11:00."

Kyle: "So the murder happened BEFORE Craig ever contacted you that evening?"

Megan: "Yes, it would seem so."

Kyle: "So isn't it possible that he killed Brooke. Then to make Axel look like the killer to you, he called you with this ruse of his own."

Megan: "I don't believe that."

Kyle: "I understand your beliefs, but is it POSSIBLE that he killed Brooke, then called you and pulled this stunt to try to convince you that Axel killed Brooke."

Megan: "It is physically possible … but I don't believe it."

Kyle: "Is it fair to say that your relationship with Craig has influenced your beliefs about this case. That is, if this was a stranger, and these same facts were presented, would you believe he was guilty?"

Megan: "I don't know."

Kyle: "Thank you for that honest answer. So you DO put some weight on Craig's claim of innocence and his explanation… You trust him?"

Megan: "Yes, I trust him."

Kyle: "Detective McDowell, the lead detective, does not have this trust in Craig. He only trusted the evidence he found… and he came to conclusion that Craig is guilty… Might your judgment of the EVIDENCE be clouded by your TRUST in your partner? … …I don't need an answer to that one..." (Kyle pauses to let it sink in).

Kyle: "You are close with Craig. Does this give you motive to lie for your friend and partner?"

Megan: "You can say there's motive, but I am not lying."

Kyle: "When Craig was blackmailing Brooke for sex, were you aware he was doing it?"

Megan: (getting noticeable uncomfortable) "Yes."

Kyle: "And did you do anything about it? …It was clearly illegal. Did you tell report what he was doing?"

Megan: "No."

Kyle: "So you kept your partner out of trouble for a fairly serious crime?"

Megan: "It's not the same thing."

Kyle: "Please answer the question."

Megan: "Yes, I kept him out of trouble."

The prosecution is done with this witness. The defense has a few more questions to add:

Artie: "When you first saw all of the evidence against Craig, what did you think?"

Megan: "At first, I thought he was guilty just like everyone else."

Artie: "So your trust in Craig was not blind and absolute as the prosecution may have had us believe... What changed your mind? Did you just start to just trust him again, or was there evidence."

Megan: "He gained my trust back by explaining piece by piece how the evidence against him was faulty. It really could've been planned by Axel. And it all made sense. Axel created an opportunity to frame Craig, and he did a good job."

Court is adjourned for the weekend.

Chapter 9

A Fresh Start

Axel is very upset by what he's seen. The next day after Megan's testimony, most television surveys report that about 80% of the people think Craig is guilty. That is 10% less than before. That means one out of every ten people Axel encounters now thinks he is the serial killer. This isn't the low profile Axel likes to keep. He knows the television cameras will soon be following him wherever he goes. He tells Vicky they are moving... very soon. But he starts thinking, 'Where can I go? This trial coverage is everywhere.'

Vicky tells him, "I may have an idea. When we were driving back from Vegas, about an hour outside of Vegas, I saw a sign for 15 acres of desert land for $40,000. You recently came into $80,000, and for this cheap of a price, it has to be the middle of nowhere. Think about it, no-one will know where you are... completely secluded from the media ... ... nobody would hear our victims' screams."

Axel admits it's a great idea. Vicky tells him the phone number she memorized from the sign. Axel calls and introduces himself as Hugh Johnson. The old man who answers explains that the property is so cheap because it's so far from anything; the 15 highway runs through empty desert, far from any towns. Then you have to turn off onto a dirt road and drive about 20 minutes before you come to the near edge of the property. There's a small two room cabin at about the center of the property, but it hasn't been kept up. There are no public utilities that far out. But there's a generator there for electricity and it'll power the air conditioner. And there's a pump for underground water, but there isn't much water pressure. It's completely off the grid. (Perfect). The old man used to use the land to take his sons off-road motorcycle riding, and they had dune buggies, but the kids are grown and the land is just not being used.

Axel tells him it sounds perfect, and they set a time to meet at the cabin the next day. Axel gets directions and tells the old man to bring the deed – that if he likes the property, he'll pay cash on the spot.

Axel realizes that this old man will be the only person who knows he's there, so he disguises himself for the meeting. He wears a blonde wig and baseball cap, uses a fake blonde moustache and beard, and wears large sunglasses for the meeting. He considered just killing the old man, but someone might know he was coming out to the cabin and drive out to check on him.

The cabin is perfect for Axel's needs. As you walk in the front door, there is a main room that is fairly large. The kitchen area is part of this room but off to the right side. As you walk straight back through the main room, there's a doorway that leads to a good-sized bedroom. Once in the bedroom, there is a bathroom to the right. That's the whole place, maybe 800 – 900 square feet.

He pays the man the $40,000 cash and has him sign the deed over to Hugh Johnson. Axel has no intention of recording the deed, just using the land undisturbed.

Axel uses most of the rest of his money to fix up the cabin, and buy 'supplies'.

Back in LA, Artie meets with Craig over the weekend.

Artie: "Craig, as I told you going in, we don't have a strong case here, but Megan might have convinced one or two jurors that Axel MIGHT have killed these girls and framed you. That's all we need. I want to rest our case here."

Craig: "What? I have to testify. They need to hear from me that I'm innocent!"

Artie: "The problem with that is that once you're on the stand, the prosecution gets to ask you all kinds of brutal questions… and they will. Though it's important for the jury to hear you say you're innocent, it's way too risky…

If they barrage you with accusation after accusation and you get emotional and show the slightest sign of anger, the jury will lock in on that."

Craig: "I can handle it. I want to tell my side of the story."

Artie: "Every part of your side of the story was introduced in Megan's testimony. There are no more facts to tell. She introduced the opinion that all the evidence could have been planted by Axel and you were framed. But if you take the stand just to say you didn't do it, how will you handle questions like:

138

'Craig, why did you blackmail Brooke Jensen for sex? Was that the right thing to do?'

'Craig, what was the purpose of fingerprinting you victims with their own blood?'

'Craig, your father recently committed suicide. Did he believe you were innocent?'"

Craig drops his head into his hands out of frustration and not knowing what to do.

Artie: "Craig, trust me. I've been doing this a long time. I don't know if you'll be acquitted based on what's been presented, but if you take the stand, it's more likely you'll be convicted."

Craig: "OK... I'll trust you."

So on Monday, the defense rests its case, and closing arguments begin.

Kyle, for the prosecution, runs through all of the evidence again for the jury and concludes with...

"Every piece of physical evidence is linked to Craig Carter. We're not talking about just one murder weapon at one location. If so, sure, maybe he could've been framed... Craig Carter is linked to the bat and the knife at the crime scene... a crime scene we KNOW he was at because you heard Brooke tell us in her own voice through a 9-1-1 call.

At a second location, Craig's house, there's the rope Brooke was strangles with, Brooke's blood, pictures of three other murder victims, and blood fingerprints of all four victims…

There's NOTHING that proves or even implies that Axel Simmons was EVER at Brooke's apartment, ANY of the other crime scenes, OR Craig's house. The defense's theory is a ridiculous Hail Mary and an insult to each one of ours' intelligence. It's a desperate story from a desperate, guilty man.

Craig Carter is an extremely dangerous man who tortured and brutally murdered four women… and he took pleasure in doing it.

I said it at the beginning of this trial and I am saying it again… if this man goes free (points to Craig), he WILL kill again. It could be someone you're close to next time...
Your friend… (flashes a bloody crime scene picture of Stephanie)
Your co-worker… (flashes a bloody crime scene picture of Wendy)
Your wife… (flashes a bloody crime scene picture of Jessica)
Your daughter… (flashes a bloody crime scene picture of Brooke)"

Artie, stands for the defense's closing statements. He revisits each piece of evidence and explains how 'it's possible' that each was planted by Axel Simmons and concludes with:

"I will not lie to you, Craig Carter LOOKS guilty of these crimes. There's lots of evidence against him. But you can not find him guilty in a court of law unless he's guilty BEYOND ALL REASONABLE DOUBT… You heard Officer Megan White… She's reasonable…I'm reasonable. I see that it's possible Craig was framed. There are no eyewitnesses to any of these crimes.

Ask yourself why the police didn't even investigate Axel Simmons. He was arrested with a bag of torture and murder devices and let go. Then, women were found tortured and murdered… The defendant, a police officer, saw Axel at Brooke's apartment the night she was murdered, and as you heard from Officer Megan White, Axel clearly had the time and the locksmith skills to get into my client's house and plant evidence.

It's all POSSIBLE!...

But the police never investigated Axel Simmons because they were handed my client on a silver platter... by Axel himself… If they had looked harder at Axel, perhaps I would have the contradictory evidence against him to tell you about. Then everything might not be pointing to Craig. But the police stopped looking. Ask yourself why… and, what if...

Axel may be having a big laugh at our expense right now.

Your friend and your co-worker and your wife and your daughter won't be any safer tonight if you convict Craig Carter, and Axel Simmons is not investigated. Axel could have done this. It's VERY possible."

Kyle stands for his rebuttal:

"Sure, 'it's possible', anything is possible. You can unlock every jail cell if you believe every absurd theory of how something possibly happened. Aliens came down and framed Craig. Hey, it's possible... there's millions of other planets out there that could support life... COME ON?!!!...

There is enough evidence for any reasonable person to conclude beyond a REASONABLE doubt that Craig Carter committed these four murders.

It was conclusive when the police closed the case... They also hadn't investigated Brooke's hairdresser, should they have?... Axel wasn't investigated because there was no REASON to investigate him. The cop who saw Axel at Brooke's apartment was Craig himself. Does that seem like a reliable witness in this case. You've seen the evidence, now please... find justice for these four women and their families."

The jury heads into deliberations. There's no verdict for three days. Some of the media circus is speculating this is good for the defense. Others in the circus say it's a good sign for the prosecution. Three mind numbing days of 'experts' blathering on throughout hundreds of TV stations. Surveys are conducted... you can bet on the verdict in Vegas.

Then, about the time Axel finishes equipping his new cabin, the jury comes back with a verdict.

Craig is instructed to stand for the reading of the verdict. Megan is in the courtroom along with every 'journalist' that'll fit. The judge instructs that any outbursts before, during or after the verdict will lead to jail time for contempt of court. The courtroom is silent. You can feel the tension in the air.

The jury foreman reads, "We the jury, on four counts of murder in the first degree, find Craig Carter... Guilty of all charges."... ... ...

A few days later, Craig is sentenced to the death penalty. Naturally, there will be appeals, and it will be many years until he's executed, but his fate is sealed. He's on death row.

Craig is moved to a maximum security prison with other death row inmates – the worst of the worst... and they HATE cops there. Within the first week, Craig is badly beat up by his black cell mate; he's stabbed with a shiv by a Latino inmate at the cafeteria; and he's beaten and anally gang-raped by four white inmates in the showers. He's a target, and no gang will take him in or offer any protection. The guards see him as a serial killer and a cop gone bad, so they look the other way. Craig is all alone.

Meanwhile, Axel has supplied his cabin with lots of creative things. Nobody knows he's there. Since his mug shot has been on the news coverage of the trial, Axel has dyed his hair from brown to blonde and cut it much shorter than it was before. He hasn't shaved so that he now has a mustache and beard, and he's dyed that lighter also. He picked up a pair of glasses with thick frames that are just lightly tinted glass, no prescription. Unless someone knew him or really studied his face, they shouldn't recognize him just from the news. After all, he was never live on TV, just a black and white mug shot.

The trial is over and Axel has a promise to fulfill to Vicky. All they need now is their next victim.

It's after dark, and they drive the 30 minutes down the dirt road just to get to an isolated point on the 15 highway. They head in the direction of Las Vegas (still an hour away). Axel has chloroform and a gun with him. If he finds a good victim at a rest stop and sees the opportunity, he'll take her. Otherwise, he plans to go to Vegas and abduct a call girl. That's the plan at least.

Vicky and Axel discuss how exciting it is to not have to gag their victims, to be able to hear their screams, to be able to keep them… as long as they want … and then not have to worry about leaving a body or evidence. He can bury them anywhere and they'll never be found. Axel already dug a couple holes while he was waiting for darkness to fall. And most importantly, since victims will never be found, Axel can cut ALL of their lovely throats without the cops ever discovering a pattern.

About ten minutes down the 15 highway, Axel sees a car on the side of the road. Two girls are in the car. Axel pulls over… to offer assistance.

They are college girls who ran out of gas on their way to Vegas. Amy is the blonde, and Jenny is the brunette, both cute. Their cell phones don't work this far into the desert. Axel turns on the country-boy accent and charm he's learned to fake so well. It's a non-aggressive style that makes him seem sweet and extra-helpful.

Axel knows that if he can get them even five minutes off the 15 highway towards his property… he owns them. He offers, "We're far from a gas station in both directions. It's another hour to Vegas, and at least 45 minutes back that direction before there's a gas station. I live about 15 minutes away. I've got a five gallon gas can full of unleaded you can have. I keep it as a backup since I live in the middle of nowhere, but you gals need it more than I do. That would get you to Vegas from here."

The girls are amazed at this stranger's generosity. But it's not at all beyond their skepticism; they are good-looking college girls – they are accustomed to guys doing extremely generous things for them (they are not completely aware the generosity is ALWAYS aimed at getting in their panties). They're gullible enough to believe people are just nice.

The girls put a bag each in Axel's trunk. (Axel advised them, they don't want to leave valuables unattended in a car on the side of the road). Jenny gets in the front, and Amy gets in the back of Axel's car, and they head toward his cabin. The conversation is natural for a while. The girls have no idea what's coming. They're excited to be headed to Vegas for their first time, and they just talk about their plans. Ten minutes down the 15 highway and fifteen minutes down the dirt road, Jenny asks, "I thought your place was only 15 minutes away?"

Axel clarifies, "I meant 15 minutes off the highway. We'll be there any minute. You girls are so much fun to be around. When you get to Vegas you have to check out the top of the Stratosphere…"

The girls are still ok. The stratosphere suggestion leads their conversation to a few other sights they want to see. Even after running out of gas, and this detour, they're still in a good spirits.

…Ten more minutes go by and the car is much quieter. Both the girls are starting to feel something's wrong, but they don't know what to do. Finally Amy irrationally asks, "Could you just let us off here?... I think we should be going now."

Axel knows this is fear talking. He replies, "I can't let you out here. It's the middle of nowhere, it's pitch black outside… the rattlesnakes would get you... …Look, I know it's a little farther than I said, but I do have a place up here. I'll get you your gas and you'll be on your way to Vegas in no time."

There's silence in the car for a minute. Jenny demands, "If you don't take us back to our car NOW, I'm going to have you arrested once we get back."

Axel knows he's only a couple minutes to his cabin, and these girls can't escape. He drops the nice-guy accent and routine. He stops the car and shows them anger for the first time, "Shut up you stupid little bitch! I'm trying to do you a favor, and you threaten me? What if I were to pull out my gun and shoot you in the mouth?"

Axel pulls out his gun and points it at Jenny in the front seat. Both girls are petrified. He hits the power locks and says, "Neither of you opens a door or you both die."

Axel keeps the gun pointed at Jenny and hands her the bottle of chloroform and a rag. He commands her to wet the rag and she reluctantly obeys. The girls both start crying and begging to be returned to their car. Axel takes the rag back, grabs Jenny, in the front seat, by the hair and holds the rag over her mouth. He makes sure she isn't faking being passed out by squeezing her hand – hard. No reaction.

Amy's freaking out in the back seat, curled up to the farthest corner of the seat by the door. Axel tucks the gun into the front of his jeans and wets the rag some more. He pulls out a hammer from under his seat and says to Amy in a relatively slow, and calm, and evil voice, "You'll be unconscious in a minute." He lifts the hammer, "You can hold this rag over your mouth and inhale, or I can beat you unconscious with this hammer… Your choice."

He tosses the rag at Amy. She's hysterical, and she's hesitant to move at all. Axel lifts the hammer in a threatening motion and

Amy gives in. She cries "Wait!" and puts the rag to her face, and noticeably inhales. A few seconds later, she's completely sedated.

Axel continues to his cabin with the girls knocked out. Vicky appears, "I call the blonde… you can play with the brunette." Axel grins.

At the cabin, Axel carries the girls and their stuff inside. He's previously fashioned a dungeon in the back bedroom. The windows are boarded up. There are chains with cuffs attached to the walls to restrain a victim at the wrists and ankles. There's a bed with a sturdy metal headboard and baseboard and handcuffs already attached at all four corners. There are other items around the room designed to restrain a woman in a fixed pose.

Vicky wants to play with Amy first, so Axel attaches Jenny to the wall with the chains. The chains extend from the very top of the wall and are about two feet long. There are cuffs to put her wrists into. She's now hanging, lifelessly suspended from her wrists. Her feet touch the ground where two more restraints, with about 9 inches of chain, are attached to her ankles. She'll be able to stand on her feet when she wakes up, and will be able to more her arms and legs just a little. Axel also puts duct tape over Jenny's mouth.

Vicky requests Amy on the bed on her knees, bent forward – doggie style. Axel drops Amy on the bed face down. He attaches her ankles to cuffs coming from the bed's corners. He wraps rope around the bottom of the bed and over the back of her knees and ties it tight. He lifts her upper body up so that she's standing onto her knees. Axel puts some large pillows in front of Amy, up to her waist, and lays her forward onto them. That positions her with her ass raised in doggie position. Then Axel fully extents her arms towards the front corners of the bed and uses rope to tie her arms in place – there's a couple feet of rope extending from her wrists to the very top of the metal bedpost. She's stretched out, forward and out to the corners of the bed. Amy is tied tight enough that her arms and chest are suspended in the air, over the bed, from the pillows that are supporting her waist. She has no room to move at all. Since she's still unconscious, her head is dropped down, but it doesn't reach the bed. Axel leaves Amy's mouth uncovered.

Axel has left the girls fully clothed for now. He wants their reaction as he cuts the clothes off of them. While he patiently waits for the girls to wake, he goes through their stuff. One bag has $2600.00 and the other bag has $4200.00. Axel is pleased and makes a mental note to himself: it is better to abduct women driving towards Vegas than away from Vegas.

Amy and Jenny wake up. Jenny's producing some very muffled screaming sounds and is kicking out with her feet as hard as she can against the chains. She has several inches of play to go back and forth, but she can only hurt her ankles; those chains are very sturdy in the wall. Amy can't move, but she can scream, "HELP! Somebody Help Us! Please! He's gonna kill us!..." (etc... the usual stuff)

Axel takes Amy's picture from the front of the bed so he can see her face. Then he walks over to Jenny, reaches under her shirt with a knife, and cuts off her bra from between her breasts. He lifts her shirt up over her breasts with his left hand and takes her picture with his right hand.

Amy screams on for a few minutes. Axel just sits across the room and feeds on her fear. Finally he informs her where she is and that nobody will ever hear her. Her demeanor changes as she realizes that her calls for help are useless. She begs, "Please sir, let us go. We won't tell anybody." She's crying.

Axel takes out a large pair of heavy duty scissors. He starts at the bottom of Amy's jeans and cuts them from the back of her right ankle, up her calves, to the side of the rope at her knee, up her thigh, past her ass, and through the top - then the other leg. He cuts off her shirt, her panties and then her bra. Since her upper body is suspended, her breasts drop down and hang in the air from her chest. They're each a good handful. Amy continues to cry and beg, but Axel has no sympathy - it only encourages him.

Jenny can only watch as this is all happening to her friend.

Amy is completely naked and bent over. Axel calls out to Vicky, who's not in the room, "Hey Vicky. What are you doing? ...She's ready for you."

Axel doesn't know what Vicky has planned, but he takes a seat a few feet from the bed, knowing it'll be fun to watch. Vicky enters the room from the bathroom. She's completely naked except for a strap-on protruding from her pubic area. This is

NOT some dainty little strap-on with a little 6 inch pink plain-looking phallus. It's a LARGE 12 inch BLACK dong, shaped very much like a real penis with veins and balls and detail. It's very thick and has some weight to it. Axel says, "Damn Vicky, you DO have penis envy!"

Vicky responds with, "Axel, even you should have penis envy of this thing."

Vicky approaches Amy from behind. She stops for a moment to look over her prey. Vicky spits in both hands and rubs it on the black dong. She mounts Amy's pussy and pushes this monster dong hard into her. Amy takes it all without a problem. Vicky fucks her for a while, smacking her ass as she goes and taunting things like, "You like my huge cock, don't you, you filthy whore." Vicky is certainly enjoying herself.

For a brief moment while this is going on, Axel gets a dizzy spell and sharp headache. This episode is accompanied by one of those fleeting smells... It smells like... Danielle? Not just her perfume, the total smell that was Danielle – her perfume, her hair products, the scent of her skin and a trace of her pussy. After a moment it's gone. That was a weird one.

Axel recovers and watches Vicky some more. After a while Vicky tells Axel, "Come over here and cut her while I'm fucking her... I wanna see some blood."

Axel picks up a large pocket knife, unfolds it and approaches. Amy was begging and crying while Vicky was fucking her, but as Axel approaches with a knife, she gets much more hysterical.

151

Axel cuts through flesh, about a quarter inch deep, from Amy's right shoulder, down her back, and all the way down to her right ass cheek. Blood spills out all over the place. Amy screams in pain now. Jenny's eyes get very wide with panic and she cries harder. Axel makes a similar cut all the way down Amy's left side. These wounds are painful, but they're not at all fatal. Axel sits back down to watch. The blood has turned Vicky on even more; she fucks Amy even harder.

Vicky reaches below her black balls and rubs her own pussy while continuing to thrust in and out of Amy. With the blood, and Amy's screams of fear and pain, it doesn't take long before Vicky brings herself to a very strong orgasm.

When she's satisfied, Vicky says to Axel, "I'm going to give her a 'Bloody Sanchez.'"

(If you don't already know what a 'Dirty Sanchez' is, go look it up on the internet... I can wait).

Vicky pulls out her big black dick from Amy and rubs the tip of it all over Amy's back, so that it's dripping with blood. Vicky struts to Amy's face and rubs the tip across Amy's upper lip – a blood mustache – a Bloody Sanchez.

Axel, still sitting, claps his hands, "Bravo!"

Vicky takes a bow, black dong waving in the air, dripping Amy's blood. Vicky says, "I'm done with her. Do you want to keep her, or should we kill her?"

Axel replies, "This blonde is your toy. It's up to you."

Vicky says deviously, "...I say we kill her."

152

Axel walks back over to the left side of the bed with the large pocket knife and puts his right knee on the bed. He moves his right hand with the knife to Amy's neck and holds the blade to her throat. Vicky strattles Amy's bloody back and puts her hand over Axel's hand on the knife handle. Amy is crying and pleading for her life, "Please!... Please, please don't kill me!... I'll do anything!"

Axel and Vicky together cut deep into her throat. Blood pours out of the wound and Amy's head drops limp from her neck... She's gone.

Axel takes his 'after' picture. He cuts the ropes that held her wrists and knees in place. He unlocks the cuffs on her ankles and takes her fingerprints with her blood. Jenny's watching in shock from what's happened. Axel rolls Amy's body off the right side of the bed and she drops onto the floor with a 'thud.'

Axel douses a rag with chloroform and approaches Jenny. He spontaneously gets an idea for a cruel game. He puts the rag down and offers, "Jenny, I'm going to make you an offer. I'm going to cut off your clothes and open the front door. You have a chance at freedom if you can run fast enough. You'll have a 30 second head start. Nod if you want to play along." She nods up and down briskly.

Axel enjoys the hunt as much as the kill. It's like foreplay. Axel removes her shoes and cuts off her jeans, shirt, bra and panties. He removes the tape over her mouth and unlocks both her ankles and then her left wrist. With her right wrist, he says "Time starts …now."

There are weapons all over the place, and on her dash for the door, Jenny grabs a large hunting knife and runs for her life, completely naked.

Axel walks to the front door to see where she's heading. He honors the 30 second head start, but keeps a flashlight pointed at her. The dumb chick picked the wrong direction and is running the wrong way down the dirt road, away from the highway – nothing buy even more desert that way.

After 30 seconds, Jenny is not very far at all. Axel has put more chloroform on the rag and runs at full sprint. Besides being much faster, he has the advantage of shoes. Axel catches up to Jenny within 100 yards and tackles her with all of his body weight on top of her. Axel slides on top of Jenny on the gravelly ground for about 5 feet. Jenny is bloodied all across her arms and legs and belly and tits from road rash, and her feet are bloody from running barefoot. Axel keeps his weight on top of her and forces the rag over her face. She holds her breath and wants to stab him with the knife, but she can't get her arm free. Finally, Jenny succumbs and passes out…

Jenny wakes up in the same position Amy was in: naked on the bed, completely restrained in doggie position, arms extended, and chest suspended in the air by her arms. Her breasts are larger than Amy's, and they hang down enough that her nipples just barely touch the bed.

As Jenny comes to, she's panicks as she realizes her position. And making it even more horrifying and surreal is that the bed is already covered in blood, and her dead friend is within her vision on the floor to her right.

Axel's been waiting for her to wake up. The large hunting knife Jenny chose is lying on the right side of the bed. Jenny thinks she knows what she's in for and starts balling her eyes out. She knows it's futile, but she begs for her life. Axel loves this display and undresses himself. He's already aroused. No condom needed. He walks behind Jenny.

It's Vicky's turn to watch, and she's seated about 5 feet away to the right side of the bed. She's made some popcorn. She sees Axel's erection and chimes in, "Hey Axel... Are ya sure ya don't wanna to use the strap-on?"

Axel points his cock, alternating up and down, between Jenny's vagina and asshole, and says, "Eenie... meenie... mienie... mo... ...I tried... to let... Jenny... go... ... but she... ran... way too... slow... ...eenie... meenie... mienie... MO" (he landed on her ass).

Axel shoves his dick into her ass. Jenny lets out a high pitched squeal – Axel was NOT gentle about it. This isn't just anal sex; this is a rough ass-fucking. Jenny's screaming in pain... and the knife hasn't even come into play yet.

Axel leans forward, reaches around, and grabs at her swinging tits. When he pulls back his hand, it's bloody from her road rash. This pleases him. Vicky is loving the show while crunching away at her popcorn across the room.

Axel continues to bang away at Jenny's ass, when he sees something in his peripheral vision in the room to his left. He looks over, but nothing is there. But the flash looked like it was… Danielle?

Axel ignores what he thinks he just saw and picks up the knife and makes a few slashes into Jenny's back. He then jabs the point of the knife into the top, fleshy part of her right ass cheek while he's still fucking her ass; he wants to see more of her blood. He directs some of the blood-flow with his hand, down her ass crack and onto his dick. It gives the illusion that his dick is causing her ass to bleed, like it's a weapon. Axel really gets off on this image. He was going to keep Jenny for a few days, but he's overriding his previous decision. He's about to cum. Axel keeps thrusting into her ass. He pulls Jenny's hair, back towards him, hard. Her head lifts back, and the front of her throat is fully vulnerable. Axel rests the blade on Jenny's throat for a moment. She screams from the hair pulling and continues to scream as she feels the cold blade meet her throat. Axel pulls the blade back and to the right, and slices her throat, and cums in her ass. Jenny's screaming stops. She goes limp. She's dead.

Axel looks over to Vicky, and she's smiling a twisted little smile. Axel begins to slowly remove his cock from Jenny's ass.

*As a note: sometimes when people die, their bowels relax, and whatever may be in there is released (they shit their pants… if they're wearing pants). Keep in mind, this girl not only just died, she was roughly ass fucked, and afraid for her life (…and she had two Jack In The Box tacos for dinner).

What happens next can only be described as an ASS EXPLOSION!

As Axel removes his cock from Jenny's ass, a spray of shit splatters Axel from his knees to his chest. It's accompanied by a very rude sound… and smell. Axel's virtually paralyzed looking down at the mess. His mouth is hung open and his eyes are wide as his brain tries to process what just happened.

Vicky, from across the room, is also stunned for a couple seconds. She stops chewing on her popcorn as she takes in the situation. After the couple seconds though, she has an involuntary, yet decisive reaction… laughter. First just a little, but it builds quickly and uncontrollably:

"ha………….. ha …………… ha ……………. ha …….. ha …….. ha …… ha ……ha …ha …ha ..ha ..ha .ha,ha,ha,ha,ha"

Axel is NOT amused. He was calm, but Vicky's initial laughter starts to make him angry. His brain catches up as follows: 'She's laughing AT me - that's making me angry. I'm covered in shit - that's making me angry. She's laughing AT me BECAUSE I'm covered in shit. I am furious!'

157

Tears come to Vicky's eyes from the hilarity. She actually doubles over and brings herself to the ground because she's laughing so hard.

Axel has turned his head to look toward Vicky, but other than that, he's not moved his body at all, just frozen in place.

But his rage peaks and completely dissipates after a few seconds. Watching Vicky laughing so hard has actually lightened his mood. Her laughter is infectious, and Axel himself slowly starts to laugh at his situation.

Vicky tries to compose herself; still on the ground, she wipes the tears from her eyes and stops laughing for a split second.

Axel looks down and a blob of shit plops off of his still erect penis and hits the floor with a 'splat' sound...

Vicky loses it again, laughing uncontrollably. Axel, who's also laughing pretty hard now too, wipes his thigh with his hand and hurls shit across the room at Vicky, who's still on the floor. It splatters her, and she's disgusted, but she can't stop laughing still.

In about the last minute, Axel's emotions have taken a rollercoaster ride. First he was excited and satisfied, (he just murdered his victim and had an orgasm). Then he was startled and confused (by the shit-storm). Then he was in a deep rage. And finally, uncontrolled laughter. All this, in about 60 seconds!

And then Axel has an epiphany, a very strange realization... He has fallen in LOVE with Vicky!!!

Axel cleans himself up, takes Jenny's picture, and finger-prints her. He drops the two college girls, and their possessions, in a hole that he dug earlier - about 20 yards from the cabin. He'll fill it back up with dirt in the morning when there's day-light.

Axel doesn't say a word to Vicky about his new found feel-ings. He doesn't know how she might react to this type of information. But he does ask Vicky again what happened to Danielle. Vicky just says that she's in a better place. That does not comfort Axel... at all.

Chapter 10
A Love Story / Things Get Wierd

Axel sleeps in the front main room of the cabin in a bed that doesn't have restraints. The back room, technically the bedroom, is for his guests.

Axel goes to bed alone. He doesn't know where Vicky goes at night; he hasn't seen her sleep. But in the morning, as he wakes up, Vicky is lying in his arms. She's warm - it feels nice. Does she know what Axel was thinking the night before?

As Axel is becoming more awake and alert, he notices that he can hear the shower water running. He gently nudges Vicky to the side (she does not wake) and walks through the back bedroom and into the bathroom to investigate. He's wearing only a pair of boxers. Axel opens the shower curtain with a fast motion... He sees Danielle, naked, soaking wet, and holding a large chef's knife – just like the one Vicky cut her throat with! It's almost like the movie Psycho in reverse. Danielle is pale and still has the large slit across her throat, and it's still bloody.

Danielle says to Axel in a demanding tone, "Why did you kill me VICKY?!!!"

Axel is completely confounded by this statement and says out loud, "What? What are you talking about?..."

Axel has more cognitive dissonance as he realizes to himself, 'that sounded like Vicky's voice coming out of my mouth???'

Axel glances downward at himself and sees... a woman's form... He still has on his boxers, but he sees breasts, and a smooth, hairless, curvy woman's body. He looks to his left at the bathroom mirror and sees Vicky staring back at him. He's stunned; it feels like he's in a dream – it's completely surreal. Axel continues to look in the mirror and touches his face, Vicky's face, to corroborate what he is experiencing. As he's staring into the mirror, Danielle lunges and thrusts the knife into his right temple. It penetrates into his head several inches.

As the knife pierces his head, Axel can't feel it, but he sees it happening in the mirror. And once it's lodged through his skull, into his brain, he sees his face morph from Vicky's face, back into his own. He stares in the mirror at the knife sticking out of his own head and some blood trickling from the knife down the side of his face. He touches the blood with his finger and looks at it – real blood is on his fingers. After a couple seconds of intense confusion, Axel falls to the ground and has a seizure. It's a strong seizure that lasts about a minute.

Axel re-awakens on the bathroom floor and slowly stands. Danielle is gone. His reflection looks like his own. He carefully checks his head in the mirror and touches all around his right temple with his fingers. There's no sign his head was ever stabbed. There's no blood on his finger or on the floor. He looks down and checks over his body. It is HIS body: hairy... (check), no breasts...(check), penis... (CHECK!!!).

161

Did he sleepwalk? Was it a dream? Vicky is still in his bed sleeping, she wasn't wakened through this whole episode. Axel climbs in bed under the covers, spoons with her, and everything seems OK. Vicky wakes as he cuddles her. She's facing away from him as the little spoon. She opens her eyes and says, "Axel… I had a dream… We were in love… It was nice… Really nice… Then Danielle came out of nowhere and killed you. She thought you were me, and she stabbed you in the head with a knife… … What do you think it means?"

Axel is bewildered, "Did this happen in the cabin's bathroom?"

Vicky replies, "No… It definitely wasn't here. It's a little foggy, but I think it was in a car."

They lay in bed for a little while, but Vicky can't sleep. She's wide awake staring at the wall across the room. She has something on her mind. She 'coincidentally' realized she was in love with Axel last night too. She floats an idea, "Axel… do you wanna have sex?"

Axel opens his eyes, he wasn't asleep, but he was drifting off. That statement got his full attention. "Is that something we can do?"

Vicky replies, "I do have a vagina… You've got a penis… You can feel me against you body, right?"

Axel: "Yeah, you feel good… You smell good… You seem real… But you're dead."

Vicky replies jokingly, "Is that it? You draw the line at necrophilia?"

Axel: "No… Yes... I mean… I didn't mean it that way. You're not dead like that."

Axel ponders the idea, "If I were a necrophiliac, I could be having a threesome in a hole with two college girls right now."

Vicky says, "Well I'm positive I'm a better lay than both of those girls combined."

She rolls over to face Axel and goes in for a kiss. Axel reciprocates; it's a very passionate kiss. Axel moves to nibbling her earlobe and kissing her neck. He's acutely aware that he's kissing bruises on her neck that his hands are responsible for. Their clothes quickly come off, and Vicky climbs on top of Axel and puts him inside her.

Axel is also well aware, from their encounter ten years ago, that Vicky likes it rough. But now he loves her and isn't being aggressive. After a little while, she tells him to spank her ass. Axel is happy to comply.

Vicky has a loud orgasm and then says she wants him on top of her, so they switch positions. They're going at it for about 45 minutes – Axel can't cum. He feels love for her, but can't cum without the violence. Vicky realizes this too.

Vicky says seductively, "Choke me."

Axel is afraid he'll kill her again. He keeps fucking her, as if she never said it. Vicky repeats a little stronger, "I want you to choke me!" And she moves his hand onto her throat.

Axle is looking at how his hand is now exactly covering the bruises already on her neck. The only difference from ten years ago is that her hair, in the backdrop of his hand, is now black instead of red. He wants to squeeze, but he knows he shouldn't. Vicky starts to build to another climax and now demands, "Choke me!... Squeeze!... Now!"

Axel does squeeze. He watches her face turn red and her orgasm build. This was exactly what Axel needed – he starts to cum too. He's been cutting off Vicky's air for too long now, but he's cumming inside her. Vicky pulls at his hand, but once again, Axel doesn't let up until after she's stopped struggling.

Axel looks into her still open eyes and sees she's dead. He lets his body fall flat on top of her, his forehead resting on the pillow to the side of her head. She's not breathing; she's still warm, but she's dead. Axel couldn't stop himself, but he's now distraught over what he's done.

He starts to cry with his face dug into the pillow. A minute goes by, and he now feels Vicky, beneath him, take a breath. Axel's optimistic for a moment and lifts his upper body to look at her face and confirm she's alive somehow.

But it's not Vicky anymore... It's Danielle. She doesn't have the knife wound on her neck anymore. Instead, on her neck, the wound is replaced by finger-shaped bruises. She isn't pale anymore; she's breathing. She's fully alive.

Axel jumps off of her and off of the bed – fearful - as if he saw a ghost. Danielle slowly fades away and disappears right in front of his eyes. Axel spends the next several hours wondering if Vicky's really gone this time. He's extremely sad and mad at himself for choking her for so long. He's a serial killer; remorse is not something he's accustomed to.

Axel files Amy and Jennifer's pictures and fingerprints away and fills in their grave with dirt. The irony crosses Axel's mind that he's now killed Vicky twice but doesn't have any blood fingerprints to show for it.

As Axel is eating dinner that evening, Vicky walks through the front door of the cabin – like some sort of twisted magician. But now, her hair is a dark shade of red again! - like when he met her in Atlantic City.

She doesn't seem angry, but Axel apprehensively watches and waits for her to talk first. Vicky sits at the table and just stares at Axel's face without saying a word. Once again, she knows how to make him uncomfortable.

Finally Axel asks, "Are you OK? Are you pissed?"

Vicky playfully says, "For what?"

Axel replies, "Well, I didn't make enough franks and beans for you… And also, by the way… I strangled you to death! … again!"

Vicky finally lets him off the hook, "Axel, don't worry about it… Really… I told you to choke me… I'm fine."

Axel asks, "What about your hair?"

Vicky: "I decided to try being a redhead again. What do you think?"

Axel: "I like it. I like it both ways, red and black... you remind me a little of Officer Trixie when you have red hair."

Over the next several days, Vicky and Axel are like a typical couple in new love. They eat together, laugh, reminisce about Axel's exploits, and have sex two or three times a day. The sex is rough, but Axel doesn't have to kill her to be able to cum anymore.

On day five, Vicky is getting her appetite for blood back. She talks Axel into abducting another victim for them to play with. They agree that there shouldn't be a string of victims going missing along the highway, so they decide to go all the way to Vegas to grab a call girl.

Axel packs his gun, chloroform and other supplies, and they decide to leave after the sun sets. They're going to be in the car for a while, so Vicky asks if she can bring along Axel's fingerprint collection to reminisce more about his victims. Axel agrees it'll be a good way to pass the time on the highway. And once on the road, each turn of the page is another captivating and unique story of Axel's brutality. He's not shy about the details. It's like foreplay for Vicky. Her panties are completely soaked through by the time they can see the bright lights of Las Vegas in the distance.

Once in Vegas, Axel gets a paper, and together with Vicky, they select 'Kinky Kimmy'. Her ad says 'I'm Flexible'. Axel likes her because, in her picture, she's standing on one leg, and her other leg is straight up, so that her calf is by her face; he can bend her, and then he can break her. Vicky likes her because she has long blonde hair and really big full breasts.

Axel calls Kinky Kimmy and sees how flexible she is: "I know this is a little weird, but my fantasy is to grope a total stranger. I want you to meet me behind my motel."

Axel describes his car and the location and tells her:

"Open the driver's side door; there will be $1000.00 on the seat. I will be in the back of the car. Take the money and sit in the driver's seat. Wear a loose shirt - no bra. If you wear a jacket or something over your shirt, take it off once you're in the car. Don't say a word – just count the cash, look forward, and let me feel you up. When I'm ready, we'll go into the motel and have sex... I assume $1000.00 will cover this specific encounter."

Kimmy thinks to herself that this is an unusual one, but she's had much stranger requests, and it seems like a fairly harmless way to start the session. She agrees and says she can be there in 45 minutes.

When Axel sees Kimmy park and begin to approach his car, he douses a rag with chloroform and holds it very low behind the driver's seat. Kimmy is wearing an unzipped black leather jacket over a very loose t-shirt, and obviously, no bra. With each step she takes, the unzipped jacket can not confine her large boobs, which are bouncing and swaying from side to side within her t-shirt.

Kimmy opens the car door, and the interior light turns on. Kimmy takes a quick peek at Axel in the back seat, picks up the cash, sits down, counts the money, puts it in her purse, takes off her jacket, and closes the car door. The interior light turns off, and it's pretty dark inside the car. Motel lights from the other side of the building and casino lights in the distance, keep the alley from being completely dark, but nobody outside of the car would be able to see anyone inside the car. Kimmy faces forward and leans back expecting hands to start groping her chest.

Axel looks around to make sure nobody else is around. He reaches his left hand over her shoulder, across her body onto her right tit. He gropes for a couple seconds and then he raises that forearm a little higher to her neck and pulls back firmly to restrain her. At the same time, he reaches around with his right hand and holds the rag over her face. She struggles for about 20 seconds, and then she passes out.

Axel gets out of the car and pushes Kimmy to the passenger's seat and quickly wraps duct take around her wrists and then around her ankles. He tips her seat back and puts a blanket over her (and the restraints), so it will appear that she's napping.

Axel proceeds to drive onto the main road. There are three lanes running each direction, and Axel is stopped at a red light; he is first in line in the far left lane. After a few seconds, a motorcycle cop has split lanes from behind and stops right next to Axel's car. The cop is just a couple feet from Kimmy, and he looks down at her from his upright position. Kimmy is reclined and motionless with her eyes closed. She looks like she's either sleeping or dead. Axel sees the cop glancing into his car, and this makes Axel understandably nervous. Axel adjusts her blanket a little - just to give the impression that she's sleeping and he's tucking her in. The cop makes eye contact with Axel for just a second, and Axel turns back to look forward again. This light seems to be taking FOREVER to turn green... Finally it turns green and the motorcycle cop speeds ahead.

Axel continues up the highway onramp and heads towards home. He re-wets the chloroform rag; if Kimmy shows any sign of life, he can reach over and make her inhale the chemical before she realizes what's happening. Axel knows he can keep her sedated the whole way home.

Vicky is in the back seat behind Kimmy. She's reaching forward most of the drive doing what Kimmy was expecting from Axel – groping her breasts. Actually, Vicky is only groping with her right hand. She's still flipping through Axel's binder with her left hand. She asks Axel questions about girls' names and how he played with her and exactly how he killed her. She loves the pictures, especially the 'after' pictures. Vicky is seriously turned on.

Suddenly, as Axel drives along this dark highway in the middle of the desert, Danielle materializes in the back seat next to Vicky and directly behind Axel. Vicky sees her imediately, but Axel does not. Danielle has the familiar chef's knife in her right hand in her lap. Danielle is focused on Axel and glares quietly at the back of his head. Vicky says, "Axel, pull over. Danielle has a knife!"

Axel looks in his rear view mirror and sees Danielle behind him. He starts to slow down and pull to the shoulder, but Danielle lifts the knife and lunges at Axel's head with a sideways swing.

Vicky tries to grab her arm to stop her, but her hand passes right through Danielle's arm – like one of them is was ghost. Axel is looking into the rear view mirror and watches the knife penetrate into his right temple. Axel immediately goes into a seizure.

The car was slowing down, but he is still doing about 40 miles per hour when the seizure begins. The car is completely out of control and continues toward the shoulder and off the road. Past the paved shoulder is a relatively steep decline of dirt for about five feet. As the car's right wheels drop down to follow this decline, the left wheels are still high on the road. It causes the car to roll in a clockwise direction. The car skids on the desert ground on its side and then flips upside down on its roof. Finally it comes to a stop.

Kimmy is still passed out. She wasn't wearing a seat belt, so she was thrown around as the car rolled, and she is bloodied. But she is alive. Axel was wearing his seat belt, but he's having a very long seizure. It lasts through the car accident and several minutes after the car stops moving. Then he's passed out in a coma – hanging upside down.

Chapter 11

In Trouble

Axel slowly regains consciousness and opens his eyes. He's lying on his back. He sees his wrists handcuffed to the rails of a hospital bed. There are tubes coming out of his nose and a needle in his arm. To his left there are devices monitoring his bodily functions. Axel looks to the right and sees a cop standing at the doorway, presumably stationed there to guard Axel from escaping.

The cop notices Axel wake up and walks over to Axel. He matter-of-factly explains that he is in the hospital under police custody and reads him his rights. He is being charged with kidnapping and MANY, MANY counts of murder in the first degree. The cop explains that Axel has been in the coma for three days.

Axel is caught and he knows it. He felt safe keeping his collection because he knew he would never leave enough evidence for the cops to get a search warrant for his home. He didn't foresee this bizarre encounter while driving. The ironic part is Axel ensured the cops would never be looking for a serial killer at all. Instead, he essentially confessed by delivering a binder full of evidence against himself. He was his own undoing.

Kinky Kimmy's abduction supports that he must have killed all the victims in his collection - including the four women Craig was convicted of murdering. For three of those girls, Axel still has half of their fingerprints and the 'after' pictures. And for Brooke, he has everything documented in his binder.

Axel's hands are restrained; he is unable to touch his head. As he tries, the handcuffs stop his movement and make a metal clanking noise on the metal bedrails. Now, he is the captive cuffed to a bed.

A doctor enters Axel's room. Axel asks, "Hey doc, how bad's the knife wound to my head?"

The doctor answers, "The bruises and cuts from the car accident are not severe... You don't have a knife wound..."

Axel can't figure out how he woke up in the hospital. The last thing he remembers is Danielle stabbing him.

The doctor further explains, "You've been having seizures sporadically while in a coma over the last three days. We did several brain scans and found a large tumor in your brain... by your right temple. There's no telling how long it's been there, but it's definitely growing. A tumor like this could have many symptoms including these seizures... Also dizziness, headaches, sensory hallucinations ...visions, sounds, smells... It's large enough to be life threatening. If untreated, it could take a month, but most likely it'll be terminal within another week or two. During this time the seizures will get worse as the tumor grows and cuts off blood to other parts of your brain...

…The good news for you is that the tumor is in a spot that's operable. And while in police custody, they must provide medical treatment, free of charge. There's a 90% success rate of a normal life after this operation.

Once you sign the consent forms, I can reserve an operating room for tomorrow morning… I'll leave these forms for you to look over, and I'll be back soon."

The doctor leaves and Vicky walks in. Axel KNOWS she's not real now, but he still loves her. Vicky asks, "Are you going to get the operation?"

Axel replies, "I don't know... I'll die otherwise… But if I live, I'll be in jail 'til all the formalities that lead up to my lethal injection… …Kind of funny that they have to spend all of this money to cure me, just so they can spend a lot more money to kill me."

Vicky: "Ya know, they sterilize the needle before a lethal injection... Wouldn't want you to get an infection…."

After a few moments of contemplative silence Vicky adds, "You know, the operation will kill me, right?"

Axel had not thought of that until she just said it out loud. The tumor was causing hallucinations. No more tumor, no more hallucinations, no more Vicky.

Axel asks, "But you're not really here... You're not real?"

Vicky tells him, "I'm not real to the doctor or to the cops or anyone else... But I am real to you."

Vicky climbs into bed with Axel and rests her head on his chest. Some tears well up in her eyes, "Axel, I love you. I understand if you get the operation. If you don't, it sounds like we only have a few weeks left anyway."

Axel has considered his options and has made up his mind quickly: "If I get the operation, the rest of my life is hell. I'll never be free, and I'll never see you again. Why even live... If I don't get the operation I may die soon, but at least I can spend the rest of my life with you."

Vicky smiles with the tears still in her eyes, and she gives Axel a kiss on the cheek. She's sad that Axel (and her) will die soon from the tumor, but she knows that he loves her.

The next character to walk in the room is a man in a suit carrying a briefcase. He introduces himself:

"Axel Simmons, my name is Lou Clancey. I've been court appointed to represent you as your attorney... Here's what we're looking at: Kimberly Wells was found restrained with duct tape in your car with chloroform in her system. She's testifying that you kidnapped her. The police found a binder in your car that had fingerprints in blood of 135 women, all confirmed to have been murdered over the last 10 years... all except two: two college girls missing for about a week. Your binder has photos of all the girls, dead at the crime scenes, including these college girls, so these girls' families are being notified that they were murdered.

If you have an explanation for the contents of this binder, I'll work on a defense. But the best I may be able to do based on what they have is to try to work out a deal that would have you in a mental institution for life instead of a maximum security prison... or the death penalty... Do you have any explanation?"

Axel knows he will be dead soon from the tumor, long before any trial could convict him. He pauses and tells Lou, "...Yes, I do have an explanation... Over the last ten years I tortured and murdered those women – what did you say the count was, 135? I lost count at some point... I framed Craig Carter for four of those murders, and I was going to kill Kinky Kimmy or Kimberly Wells or whatever her name is... That's my explanation."

Lou is taken aback by the frank confession, "Would you like me to prepare an insanity defense and try to make a deal that would have you committed to an insane asylum? It sounds like you need help."

Axel replies, "I'll be dead long before that. The doctor said I have at most a month."

Lou: "I was told that they can remove the tumor and you should fully recover."

Axel: "But I'm not getting that operation. Why try to live? What do I have to look forward to?"

Lou: "So what do you want me to do? Do you want a trial, or do you just want to plead guilty?"

Axel has had enough of this guy and says strongly, "I don't fuckin' care... Thanks for your services... You can go now!"

Lou exits, and the cop at the door walks back in. He over-heard the conversation and adds, "You know, the families of the two college girls would like to give their daughters a proper bur-ial... Where are the girls?"

Axel quips, "Give me immunity for my crimes and I'll give you the two bodies."

The cop knows he will not get any cooperation and goes back to the doorway.

The story was released to the media while Axel was still in his coma. The media circus has reformed. They now report as if they were always on Craig's side when the slant was always that he had to be guilty.

It takes a couple days, but Craig's attorney, Artie, meets with Kyle (the prosecuting attorney), and with the new evidence, Kyle agrees that Craig was indeed framed by Axel. They have to go before the judge to get him released. After three more long days, the judge overturns the sentence. Craig is pronounced 'not guilty' and is released from custody. Megan is there to take him home. She is the only one who believed in him, and he is grate-ful to her. But he walks out a badly damaged man. He was abandoned by everyone; all of his friends turned on him. His fa-ther is dead. The time in prison was brutal on him, physically and mentally.

Megan tells him the captain has his gun and badge waiting for him if he still wants them. Megan takes him to his house. It's in complete disarray from when the police searched it. He's happy to be free, but his life will never be the same.

Meanwhile, a bright talented young black defense attorney watches the news and hears that Axel isn't having the operation and that he'll be pleading guilty. But he's conceived a good strategy to defend Axel that they're not pursuing. This attorney isn't focused on justice. He doesn't necessarily want Axel back on the streets, but if he's able to get Axel Simmons, The Real Fingerprint Killer, acquitted, it would catapult his career to superstar defense attorney. Fame and fortune would follow. This defense attorney's name is Connie Jockren.

Connie pays Axel a visit in the hospital to offer his services:

Connie: "Hi Axel, my name's Connie Jockren. I'm told you're represented by a public defender."

Axel: "I don't think he'll be defending me, but he was assigned to represent me."

Connie: "No offense to public defenders, but I'm a much better and more aggressive lawyer. I have a strategy that may very well get you acquitted. You could walk away a free man. And I will offer my services pro bono… Free that is."

Axel: "Why would you want to help me? …Do you think I'm innocent?"

Connie: "No. (chuckles) You should probably be drawn and quartered… Maybe publicly hanged or stoned to death… You're a living breathing monster. But it's my job to keep the judicial

177

system in check. And the system doesn't work unless ALL of the accused are properly defended in court... Plus, this is an enthralling nationally televised case. To have that stage and win a jury trial for a man who killed 135 women over 10 years would make me a living legend among defense lawyers."

Axel: "So, this should be good…what's this strategy?"

Connie describes his plan in detail to Axel. It's genius; it actually covers every legal base to give Axel a viable legal defense. It's a long-shot, but with a little luck, and the right jury, Axel believes Connie might actually pull it off.

To begin the process, Axel must start being cooperative. He must undergo psychological evaluations by several experts – for the defense and for the prosecution. He must make people believe he's a good person… starting now. And he must get the brain tumor removed! The certain byproduct of removing the tumor is killing Vicky (for the third and final time!) That makes this decision unbearable.

Before Axel has agreed to anything, Connie wraps up, "I'll leave my card here, and I'll stop back tomorrow. Fire the other attorney and don't talk to anyone else… not a word."

Vicky was lying with Axel the whole time, so she understands the situation has changed. This new defense gives Axel a new hope of freedom. And besides that new circumstance, Axel's been having stronger and stronger seizures that last longer and longer. As Axel gets sicker, Vicky is also growing weaker. She knows they both don't have much longer to live without the surgery. So she does the selfless thing and urges Axel to have the operation. Axel reluctantly tells the nurse to summon the doctor.

Axel signs the forms and the surgery is scheduled for the next morning.

As they take Axel from his hospital room to the operating room, Axel says his final goodbye to Vicky. Both are crying.

But once the anesthesiologist puts Axel under, he dreams vivid dreams and spends what seems like days with Vicky. They relive killing dozens of Axel's victims - ones from years ago that Vicky was not around for. But this time, each rape and murder is altered because Vicky is there and can fully participate. They make love to each other, at the crime scenes, in their victims' blood.

At the end of the dream, Vicky gives Axel a final kiss good-bye, and Axel wakes in the recovery room. It's been twelve hours since he was put under; the operation was a complete success. The tumor was removed, and there's no apparent long term damage to his brain.

Now it's time for Connie to work his magic. He enters a plea of 'not guilty, by reason of temporary insanity.'

The prosecuting attorney is Seth Rogers. Seth realizes that Connie's defense is absurd, but it's legally plausible – it could possibly work if a jury was gullible enough. But he won't offer a deal that lets Axel ever go free. He offers life in prison, or they go to trial and seek the death penalty. Connie wants his day in court, so the trial starts in three weeks.

Connie prepares Axel for what's to come and coaches him thoroughly on the legal aspects of his defense.

This trial is not about proving innocence. Axel and Connie haven't contested that Axel committed all the crimes he's charged with. They're essentially trying to get off on a technicality. The media circus has a true villain to focus on: an admitted serial killer of 135 women.

On day one of the trial, Axel's arms and legs are in shackles as he's brought into the courtroom; they remain shackled through the proceedings. Connie knows this is very prejudicial and strongly objects, but he loses this one. Axel is presumed to be one of the most dangerous men in the country, and they're not taking any chances of escape.

Axel also has a large scar on his head from the operation. That could go either way – the scar is scary looking, but it might invoke sympathy from the jury and help convey that Axel is a victim too. Axel's hair, (what's left on his head), is clean-cut short and is back to his natural color of brown. He's clean shaven and wearing a suit. He looks respectable – except for the shackles.

After opening arguments from both sides, the prosecution presents its case. Connie has stipulated that Axel killed all of these women, even the last two college girls whose bodies were never found. Axel did not want to give up his hiding spot, so with the duplicitous appearance of cooperation, he had earlier revealed to prosecutors that he dropped their bodies in the Pacific Ocean after he was done with them. Now their families can have some sense of closure, even if they can't bury their daughters.

So, since the prosecution didn't have to prove that Axel killed these 135 women, their case is relatively short. But they have to adequately paint a picture to show Axel for the villain he is, and they have to make the jury afraid to let him go. Seth presents a slide show to the jury with all of Axel's 'after' pictures along with his blood fingerprint collection. Lots of crime scene photos are shown to the jury to show the extent of the carnage. Several family members of victims give teary testimony to exemplify that these were real people before they were mutilated corpses – 135 real people that were loved by somebody. The judge limits all of this to a few days to save the court some time – this evidence could take months to present otherwise.

Seth next calls Megan White, for the prosecution, to explain how Axel framed Craig Carter for four of his murders. While she's on the stand testifying against Axel, Axel stares intensely. He's captivated by her.

Axel's been heartbroken over his loss of Vicky. He's been depressed and doesn't feel any motivation to go on. Even the prospect of being free and eventually killing again doesn't seem as thrilling without Vicky there to share it with.

But Megan's resemblance to Vicky has made Axel's fragile brain spin. He begins to equate Vicky with Megan, Megan with Vicky. He was attracted to 'Trixie' in the first place because of her resemblance to Vicky. Axel watches as Megan testifies against him. Her demeanor clearly shows her disgust and hatred towards Axel. But Axel is now drawn to her – an obsession.

The prosecution calls Kimberly Wells to the stand, Axel's only living victim. She's a very sympathetic witness. She starts sobbing as she recalls how she would be victim number 136 now if not for Axel's seizure.

The prosecution has done all that it can do. The jury knows what Axel has done in gory detail; they have sympathy for the victims; and they are afraid of what Axel is capable of. Every member of the jury detests Axel at this point... But the defense hasn't presented its case yet.

Connie has an certain intangible charisma, even when he asks unpleasant questions. Juries tend to like him.

Once the prosecution rests, Connie calls Axel's brain surgeon to the stand. The doctor has maintained a professional detached doctor/patient relationship with Axel. He is not at all on the side of letting Axel go, but he has to testify about the nature of the tumor.

Connie: "Doctor, you removed a large tumor from Axel Simmons' brain. Is that correct?"

Doctor: "Yes, that's correct."

Connie: "What types of symptoms could a tumor like this cause?"

Doctor: "Well, Axel was in a coma from it. He was having seizures sporadically that got more intense as the tumor grew. Axel claimed to have sensory hallucinations that are consistent with a brain tumor in this part of the brain..."

Connie: "Was Axel seeing and interacting with people that weren't really there?"

Doctor: "Yes, I believe he was."

Connie: "So you can safely say Axel lost touch with reality?"

Doctor: "I suppose so, to a certain extent. But he was able to hold a job. He was able to..."

Connie: "Thank you doctor. You don't need to finish... ...Could a tumor like this change someone's behavior dramatically. Change it so much that they do things they'd NEVER have done... in their right mind."

Doctor: "Sure."

Connie: "Is it POSSIBLE that this tumor could cause homicidal tendencies?"

Doctor: "This brain tumor could have adverse effects on mood, perception, logic, impulse control... It's very unpredictable how exactly it affected Axel."

Connie: "But it's POSSIBLE this tumor could have caused brutal homicidal actions?"

Doctor: "It's possible. ... But I'm not saying I think that's what happened here."

Connie: "I know. We're just establishing what COULD have happened...

...Doctor. Do you know when this tumor first developed in Axel's brain?"

Doctor: "There's no way to tell when it first developed."

Connie: "Could it have been there ten years ago?"

Doctor: "It's unlikely."

Connie: "But is it possible that Axel has suffered from this tumor... even his whole life?"

Doctor: "Without seeing a previous brain scan, I can't say how long it's been there."

Connie: "Is there a previous brain scan of Axel anywhere."

Doctor: "No, there isn't."

Connie: "Thank you doctor. One last question... Once a tumor like this is successfully removed – as in the case with Axel – do the symptoms persist?"

Doctor: "No, whatever problems the tumor was causing: hallucinations, seizures, mood disturbances, all disappear once the pressure from the tumor is alleviated."

Connie: "So... IF ...this tumor actually did cause Axel's violent behavior, the removal of this tumor would eradicate Axel's violent behavior."

Doctor: "Yes."

Connie: "Thank you. I'm done with this witness."

As Seth cross examines the doctor for the prosecution, he establishes that the tumor didn't NECESSARILY cause Axel to kill; lots of people have had similar tumors and never hurt anyone. But the burden of proof falls on the prosecution.

Connie next calls two different psychiatrists to testify that Axel appears to be perfectly sane… since the operation. They could find no sign of violent tendencies or disconnection with reality. (Axel knows how to seem perfectly normal when he wants to).

The prosecution establishes that these psychiatrists spent less than 12 hours each with Axel. Their conclusion is not reliable; Axel may still be dangerous. There's no way to know for sure. But again, the burden of proof falls on the prosecution.

And even though Seth was able to have his experts evaluate Axel before the trial, none were able to conclusively find that Axel was still violent. So the prosecution never calls an expert to counter the defense's psychiatrists.

Connie calls Axel to the stand. Axel takes small steps, dragging chains, as he's shackled at the arms and legs. The gruesome scar on his temple from the surgery is very prominent.
Connie: "Axel Simmons, you don't deny killing 135 women, torturing and raping most of them first?"
Axel: "No, I did it all. It seems like a bad dream now, but I did everything that Seth Rogers said I did. I am so… very… sorry." (Axel starts to mist up a little).

Connie: "Why did you do these things?"

Axel: "I can't explain it completely. I was hearing voices and seeing things that weren't there. They were telling me to do these horrible things to these innocent women. It was like I wasn't able to control my body. I was me part of the time, but other parts of the time, I was watching from within my body as someone else did these things."

(Axel has a few tears running down his face. He looks very remorseful).

Connie: "How long have you had these episodes?"

Axel: "It all started about ten or eleven years ago. I started hearing voices, but I was able to resist for a while. Then, one day, I met a woman in Atlantic City. It turned out she was a prostitute. At some point in the evening, I completely lost control, and I watched myself kill her. My hands strangled her to death. I swear, I never wanted to. It was like someone else was doing it while I watched."

Connie: "Since your operation, how do you feel?"

Axel: "I feel terrible. I'm racked with guilt, and I'm sick over these memories that are vivid, but still seem like a dream… But I think you were asking if I feel in control… and I AM in control. That operation gave me my life back. I have no doubt that I'm cured and I'll NEVER hurt anyone again."

Seth Rogers stands for his cross examination:

Seth: "Axel, this story is very convenient… You rape, torture and kill one hundred and thirty five women over the course of ten years. You immaculately clean up all of the crime scenes so that nothing leads the police to you. You meticulously frame a police officer for four of your murders... And once caught, you blame it all on a tumor... Tumor's gone, all better, time to get on with you life... Is that correct?"

Axel: "I wouldn't call it convenient. I didn't want any of this. The tumor was real. I was only caught because that same tumor caused me to have a seizure... But yes, I'm better now."

Seth: "How can this jury be sure the tumor caused you to kill? Maybe the tumor was just a separate phenomenon. How can they know if they set you free that you won't rape, torture and kill another 135 women?"

Axel: "I give my word that I don't have those feelings any more. The doctor confirmed that this type of brain tumor could have done this to me. I have full control back... And it's my understanding that I don't have to prove I am cured… You have to prove that I'm still sick…"

Seth: "That's right. I'm just giving the jury some things to think about..."

Seth: "Axel, you said part of the time you were not in control, but part of the time you were the real you. Give us an idea what the real you was like."

Axel: "I'm just a normal guy… not violent, good worker, I do the right things for the most part. A normal good citizen."

187

Seth: "And you're that guy now, the same normal good citizen you have been for the last ten years… but now in full control"

Axel: "Yes, I'm that same guy."

Seth: "Then here's a question Axel…If this version of yourself was such a good citizen, why not turn yourself in… during your lucidity… If you were in control some of the time, you could have stopped the out of control part of yourself. Why did you let the rapes and torture and murders continue… for ten years?" (Axel is flustered by this question).

Axel: "…I don't know... Maybe I'm different now in that way. I didn't feel the guilt before because it seemed like a different person doing those things. It was happening, but it didn't seem real. Now I feel the tremendous guilt. I would turn myself in now."

Seth: "You just completely changed your story. You said you were a good citizen before, but that person obviously didn't have a conscience. I see no reason to believe that you grew a conscience when the tumor was removed."

Connie stands, "OBJECTION! He's testifying his opinion."

The judge agrees, "Sustained. Please ask your questions and leave your comments out, counselor."

Seth: "Yes your honor… I'm done with this witness." (Seth sits back down).

The next day, in closing arguments, Seth sums up his case and closes with:

"135 women dead… Tortured, raped and murdered by Axel Simmons. Kimberly Wells was almost #136. And Craig Carter, a good police officer, had his life ruined by this man, victim #137. Axel Simmons doesn't deny any of this. This is all fact. He IS a serial killer!… This sick twisted sadist took finger prints with the girls' own blood. This was sport for him… for ten years. You have met some of these girls' families. Don't make them live the rest of their lives knowing their wives' or daughters' or sisters' or mothers' murders will go unpunished. Bring them some justice.

Axel Simmons is a VERY dangerous man. He got away with it for ten years. He's not cured! He's not remorseful! He wasn't temporarily insane …for ten years!!! Do you hear how silly that sounds.

Only you, the jury, can stop him from raping and torturing and killing many more women. I've shown you all the facts. It is up to you to go back into that room and stop this man from ever hurting another innocent woman."

Connie Jockren stands for his closing:

"Axel Simmons WAS a serial killer. You've seen what he's done, and it's horrifying. But just because he did it, doesn't mean he's responsible for it. And it doesn't mean that he's still a danger to society.

This is what's responsible (Connie holds up a jar filled with liquid and at the bottom – Axel's brain tumor).

189

This is real. You can lock it up in prison or stick a lethal injection into it. This tumor created pressure on Axel's brain causing voices and visual hallucinations. It cut off blood to parts of his brain. It caused seizures. It distorted his perception of reality. It almost killed Axel... He is a victim here too – call him victim #138. This tumor caused Axel to not be in control of his own actions... and therefore, not legally responsible for his crimes.

It doesn't matter if it was for ten years or ten minutes! The entire length of time this tumor altered Axel's behavior is the very definition of temporary insanity... Then Axel gets surgery... BAM ... no more insanity...

Ladies and gentlemen of the jury... you don't even have to definitively believe that this tumor caused Axel to kill, so your job is easy. If you even DOUBT that he was in full control of his actions, you have to find him not guilty. The judge will instruct you of this. And the doctor has told you the effect a tumor like this can have on brain function... This tumor could have taken away his control and therefore his accountability. And the prosecution has not PROVEN otherwise, not even a little, and not beyond reasonable doubt!

Don't let your emotions for the women, and the horror of theses crimes, get in the way of you upholding the law. We don't take away a man's freedom and possibly his life in this country unless we know for sure he's legally responsible... Axel is not!

And don't let the prosecution scare you. Axel is no longer a threat to society… The prosecution hasn't proven that he is. They didn't put up one expert to say that Axel is still dangerous. Wonder why?

The tumor is out of his head. The voices, and the hallucinations, and the part of him that emerged to take over and kill, are gone. There's no reason to believe that we're not left with a good man who needs a second chance.

Justice doesn't always require that someone be punished. Sometimes justice is simply that an innocent man is not further punished. If you do your job, and recognize Axel Simmons was a sick man who is now cured, you will be doing justice."

Connie sits and Seth has the last word:

"Don't fall for this…

Axel is a clever man, and his lawyer is a clever man too. You've heard how Axel covered up his crimes and framed a police officer. They came up with this defense that the surgery cured him, but don't believe it. He didn't have a conscience when he was lucid before the surgery, and he doesn't have a conscience now.

The defense claims that he was TEMPORARILY insane for TEN YEARS because of a brain tumor. This is a possible but an EXTREMELY unlikely story. Many other people get similar brain tumors and have severe symptoms, but they never hurt, rape, torture, or kill anyone. Don't let the claims that Axel is a good citizen, other than this brain tumor, have any weight. It's their whole case because there's no defense for his actions. Axel Simmons was, and still is, a dangerous serial killer…

Thank you…"

The jury is sent into deliberations.

After two days, the jury comes back with a question for the judge, and both attorneys convene in the judge's chambers: Can they find Axel criminally insane?

…They can not. Their only option for each crime is guilty, or innocent by reason of temporary insanity. Criminally insane or any lesser crime isn't an option. Both lawyers realize the jury is struggling – these twelve men and women don't want to let Axel go, but they see the tumor may be responsible.

Seth wants to make a deal. He can't bear the idea that Axel might possibly be set free. He offers 25 years in a mental facility. But Connie wants his verdict, and Axel knows he might just beat this. So they wait another day.

On day three, court is back in session. The jury has a verdict. The judge demands silence, and you could hear a pin drop, but the tension is palpable in this packed courtroom.

"We the jury, for the charges of 135 counts of murder in the first degree and 113 counts of rape… find Axel Simmons… …NOT GUILTY for reason of temporary insanity."

The judge announces that Axel is free to go and bangs his gavel and leaves the courtroom. There's shock and disbelief in the courtroom. Seth drops his head to the table. Several family members of the victims break down and start crying immediately. The room that was silent a moment ago is now completely out of control.

Axel is relieved and smiles in the courtroom for the first time. A bailiff walks over and unlocks his shackles. Connie feels and looks like he just won the lottery. He gives Axel a big hug. After the embrace, a father of one of the victims approaches Axel and sucker punches him in the face. Axel falls to the ground and the father is pulled away by the bailiffs.

Connie leads Axel out the back way of the courthouse. Axel is grateful to Connie, but Connie is equally grateful to Axel. Connie got exactly what he was after. He's a celebrity defense attorney now; he has his fame and soon his fortune.

Connie takes Axel back to his office. There's champagne and a cake waiting for them when they get there. Connie had his assistant arrange this mini-celebration. She also arranged a rental car for Axel.

After a glass of champagne, Axel asks to use a computer and Connie gives him an office to use. Axel looks up Megan White's personal information. He's become completely infatuated with her.

Chapter 12

Reckless: A New Fixation

The lead story on every news channel is about how the Real Fingerprint Killer is a free man tonight. The public is outraged. Axel knows he must stay out of sight. Everybody knows his face and everybody hates him.

After it gets dark, Axel begins driving to his hidden cabin - all of his supplies are there. He notices two police cars following him. Axel drives the speed limit and watched his rear view mirrow. Once he's beyond the L.A. County line, they turn back.

Axel makes sure nobody is following him when he turns onto the dirt road that leads to his property. He arrives at his cabin and gets some rest.

But for the following evening, he has a new plan. The operation did change him, but not in the ways he had explained on the witness stand. With the loss of Vicky, Axel is now more desperate and more reckless.

Axel packs a bag and removes every sticker from the car that gives away that it's a rental. He removes the license plates and puts on the license plates that he stole from the car outside of Vegas. This nondescript car should not attract attention now. In court, Axle was clean shaven and his hair was brown. So he re-dyes his hair blonde and puts on his fake facial hair and glasses.

He heads back to LA. There are two things he desires: Megan, and his fingerprint collection.

It's dark, and the lights are on as Axel cruises past Megan's house. She's a cop, so he has to be careful; she's not as defenseless as most of his victims, and she surely has a gun inside. Axel sneaks around the house to listen inside; He stays pressed against the outside walls, protected by the darkness. The windows are open; he hears that there are two women inside. From their conversation, he learns that it's Megan and … her sister, Rachel. He can tell from listening to them that they are very close; this makes Axel VERY happy. Axel is anxious to get a look at the sister, but he remains patiently in the darkness of the backyard for them to go to sleep.

Once all of the lights go off and about an hour more has passed, Axel quietly picks the lock on the back door. He doesn't know who is in which bedroom, so he enters the first door he comes to. He gets his first look and Rachel in the darkened room who is sound asleep in her bed. He approaches her with a chloroform rag and gently covers her mouth... but she wakes up. Axel holds her down with the rag tight to her face, but she struggles. She can't scream, but she scratches Axel's face and manages to knock the lamp off the nightstand. It makes a loud crash as it shatters. Rachel is passed out a few seconds later, but Axel knows Megan was wakened by this. He has lost the element of surprise with her. Axel picks up a candleholder that is on the nightstand. It's solid glass and has some weight to it, at least 3

195

pounds or so. He stands to the right of the doorframe so that when the door swings open, the door will block Megan's view of him. Sure enough, seconds later, Megan opens the door with her gun drawn. She flicks on the light and says, "Rachel, are you ok?" And she walks into the room toward the Rachel.

Megan sees the mess and is confused for a moment that Rachel is still asleep on the bed. Before she can spin another thought, Axel stalks forward from behind the door and clobbers her on the back of her head with the solid glass candleholder. Megan's gun goes off on impact. The bullet goes harmlessly into a wall, and Megan drops to the ground, unconscious.

This was not clean as Axel planned. The clock is ticking. A neighbor will call the police over that gunshot, and they will get here quick since Megan is a cop.

Axel takes Megan's gun and duct tapes both women at the wrists and ankles. There's no time to run up the street to retrieve his own car, so Axel looks for and finds keys in a purse in the kitchen. He opens the door off the kitchen to the garage and checks that the key fits this car… it does. He loads both sisters, still passed out, into the trunk, opens the garage door, and drives out of there as quickly as possible.

That was an adrenaline rush Axel hasn't experienced in a long time. He rarely has to improvise and rush like this. But he quickly feels at piece on the highway back towards his cabin.

Axel is well aware that there'll be no doubt the police will know he's responsible. Besides the circumstantial facts that he's (rightfully) believed to be a serial killer and has an apparent grudge against Megan for her testimony, his rental car will be found up the street. But that doesn't matte, because Axel's now in permanent hiding; he just doesn't care about blending in and maintaining a regular life anymore. He'll just have to use better disguises from now on - maybe a trip to Mexico for some plastic surgery.

About twenty minutes into the drive, Axel hears banging and muffled screaming coming from the trunk. He turns on the radio. It's pre-tuned to a country station… that won't do. He finds a rock station; AC/DC is playing, "I'm on the highway to hell…" That seems a little more appropriate. He turns it way up.

Axel arrives at his cabin. He opens the trunk with Megan's gun in one hand and a chloroform soaked rag in the other. Megan and her sister are screaming for their lives, but nobody will hear them. Since they're still restrained, Axel easily holds the rag over Rachel's mouth and them Megan's mouth, and then carries them both inside their new home.

When Megan wakes, she's naked, hanging upside down against the wall. Her ankles are in the same shackles that previously held Jenny's wrists. Megan's wrists are cuffed to the shackles on the floor. Megan can see her sister across the room. Rachel is naked, spread eagle and restrained by all four limbs with handcuffs, face-up on the bed. Rachel is not awake yet.

Axel is across the room grinding a large knife across a sharpening stone by hand. The knife is already sharp, but it's a menacing sound and Axel is part showman for his victims. Axel walks over to Megan and says, "Vicky, I'm glad to see you're awake now."

Megan responds with malice, "Who the fuck is Vicky? I thought you get off from calling me Trixie... Trixie, not Vicky, you brain-damaged, stupid fuck!... Let me out of here!"

Megan is angry and struggles with the shackles from her inverted position.

Axel informs her, "I know WHO you are, and you ARE going to play the part of Vicky from now on... I know this will take some persuading."

Axel picks up a bull whip and whips Megan's naked body twice on her belly. It stings and leaves red marks. Megan realizes she's helpless so she holds in the attitude and quiets up. Rachel starts to wake up. She's not nearly as tough as Megan. She recognizes Axel from the news and assesses her situation rapidly. She begins to cry and asks her sister, "Oh my god... Megan...Are we going to die?"

Axel responds first, "Not yet... You're not THAT fortunate."

And he puts duct tape over Rachel's mouth. He's only interested in communicating with Megan/Vicky right now. Axel slowly walks across the room back to the knife he was sharpening and then back to the bed Rachel is on. This is a show for

Axel suggests, "Really, dry?... What kind of sister are you?... You should at least spit on that big thing before ripping into her."

Megan takes the advice and does spit on the dildo. It still doesn't penetrate into her sister's pussy much. Megan pushes forward very slowly but stops after about four or five inches; she senses her sister's pain. Rachel is not at all relaxed. So, besides the mental anguish of knowing that her sister is forced to rape her, it's physically very painful for Rachel.

Axel demands, "Shove it all the way in there."

Megan gives him a dirty look, but knows better than to say anything. She complies as gently as she can. She pushes forward until it's all of the way in – about nine or ten inches, and stops. Axel instructs, "You're not done... Now fuck her.... In and out, in and out."

Megan starts pushing in and out very slowly, barely moving. Axel is getting impatient, "Vicky... I've seen you do better than that. Bang her good... She's going to be fucked hard. Either you do it right, or I will."

So Megan applies more spit to the large black dildo and gets a little more aggressive, in and out, in and out, all the while crying and apologizing to Rachel. Rachel can't even look at Megan. The humiliation is worse than the physical pain. Rachel's eyes are closed tightly, and she keeps her head turned towards the wall. She's trying to be somewhere else in her mind, but tears are streaming from her eyes.

Megan is acutely aware that Axel left this knife on the bed. She wants to pick it up and attack Axel, but Axel is out of reach, and he has a gun pointed at them. So she waits for any opportunity.

After a little while, Axel wants more. He commands, "Vicky, you should cut her flesh... Let's see some blood from this little bitch."

Megan responds desperately, "Come on, I'm doing what you asked for."

Axel insists, "I want to see her bleed. You can do it, or I can do it... I think I might cut deeper than you will... So pick up that knife and cut her... And don't stop fucking her while you do it."

Megan picks up the knife and hesitantly drags it about an inch across Rachel's belly. But it's barely a scratch. It makes a small white line, but almost no blood. Axel is not happy with this. He switches the gun to his left hand, picks up another knife with his right hand, and walks over to the sisters. He points the gun at Megan and the knife toward Rachel's chest, "This is how you make someone bleed..."

But as the knife gets close to cutting Rachel, Megan lunges towards Axel with her knife. Axel is able to jump back and get his face clear, but the knife cuts across his chest, and he fires the gun... Megan is shot in her left arm through her bicep. Her knife drops to the bed and she puts her hand to the wound. Axel's chest is bleeding, but it is just a flesh wound. Megan's in immense pain from the gunshot. The strap-on is still about six inches inside Rachel. Axel punches Megan in the face… hard. She falls to her right and off the bed. The strap-on follows and rips out of Rachel in a quick sideways painful way.

Axel says, "Let's try that again..."

He grabs Megan and forces her back onto the bed. She's bleeding from her mouth from the punch and bleeding badly from her arm from the gunshot wound. Axel presses the gun to Megan's head, "VICKY, now you're going to fuck her AND cut her for me, right?"

Axel remains right there with the gun to her head. Megan tries to gently insert the strap-on back into her sister, but Rachel's in a lot of pain there and flinches at the touch. But Megan now forces it in her. And this time, Megan cuts deep enough into her sisters belly to draw blood and makes a three inch cut.

Axel walks around and presses the gun to Rachel's head and commands to Megan, "MORE!"

So Megan cuts another line about four inches long into her sister's belly and then says, "I can't do any more… I just can't"

Axel says angrily, "You see this long cut you made across my chest." He wipes some of his blood with his hand and flicks it at Megan. "If you can do that to me, you can do it to her… Vicky… One long cut, and we'll give her a break and let her live."

Megan pleads, "It's my sister, I can't cut her like that. Don't make me. Please."

Axel has no compassion, "OK, you don't have to... I'll take care of it myself..."

Megan pressed the knife into Rachel's left shoulder – about an eighth of an inch deep. She pulls the knife toward herself, between her sister's breasts, and down to the bottom of her ribcage. It's not as deep of a cut as she did to Axel, but Axel is satisfied with this. There is lots of blood from both girls: on the girls, on the bed, on the floor.

Axel holds his knife to Rachel's throat and tells Megan, "Vicky, go lock yourself back up on the wall. You've been good, so you can have your feet on the ground this time."

He checks to make sure Megan's restraints are tight and he ties a tunicate to her arm to slow the bleeding.

Axel has procured a satellite cell phone, so he makes a call to an old friend... Craig answers. He's already aware that Megan and her sister were abducted. And he knows Axel did it. In Craig's voice is anger and urgency. Axel's voice is slow and calculated, like a true villain.

Axel: "Hi Craig."

Craig: "Axel...Where is she!"

Axel: "She's right here."

Axel presses on Megan's gunshot wound and she screams in pain.

Craig: "Did you grow another tumor? You're smarter than this... Let her go."

Axel: "I just want what's mine. I'll let her go... Just bring me my stuff."

Craig: "What stuff? I don't have any of your stuff."

Axel: "The police never returned my fingerprint collection and my photo album."

Craig: "You've gotta be kidding me?"

Axel: "Just check it out from your evidence room and bring it to me... And I'll let your partner go free. Otherwise, it's going to be fun getting acquainted with these lovely ladies... insides and out."

Craig: "Where do I bring it to?"

Axel: "Pick up my stuff and I'll call you in an hour... And Craig... This is just between us. Any sign that anyone else knows about this and I'll be mailing Megan and her sister to you in bite sized pieces for years... I may have cameras set up any-where... Understand?"

Craig: "How do I know this isn't another set-up?"

Axel: "You don't"

Axel hangs up.

Craig goes to the station and pretends that he's looking for a victim they may have missed. He reasons that if there's another woman that Axel wasn't prosecuted for, it wouldn't be double jeopardy to re-try him for the newly discovered victim. He's able to check out the evidence. But on his way out, his captain sees Craig with the binder and starts asking questions.

Even though the captain turned his back on Craig through his trial (based on the overwhelming evidence), Craig knows him to be a fair boss and a stand-up guy. So Craig tells him privately what's going on and why no-one else can be involved. The Captain does offer some help:

Captain: "He probably won't have you meet where he is keeping the girls. So here's a tracking device. It's small enough to plant behind a picture in the album so that Axel won't notice it right away."

Craig: "OK, good idea."

Captain: "Here's another tracking device. Put this clumsily in the bag. Axel will most likely check for a bug, so when he finds this he'll be less likely to continue looking."

The Captain gives him another device from his personal stash that's not police issued along with some advice. Then the conversation continues:

Captain: "Do you know what general area they're in?"

Craig: "No, they could be anywhere by now."

Captain: "OK, when you even know what city they're in, call me from your cell phone. I'll get back-up ready so once you have a location from the tracking device, you'll have help available."

Craig gets the call from Axel, "Take the 15 East. Exit anywhere in Barstow. I'll call again about the time you should be there. Don't take a police car, and don't alert the cops out this way. If I see increased activity out here, I disappear and kill your partner and her sister."

Craig heads toward Barstow in his own car. He calls the captain and tells him the direction Axel has him headed.

Axel later calls with his final instructions for Craig, "Drive another 20 miles past Barstow, there's a billboard for Cirque Du Soleil … Leave my stuff by the billboard and drive away."

Craig responds, "How do I know you won't still kill the girls?"

Axel: "You'll just have to trust me…"

Craig calls the captain while still in Barstow and tells him where he's headed. But there's still nothing the captain can do yet.

Craig leaves the bag containing the binder by the billboard – no sign of Axel around – and he drives off.

Axel is watching from far off with binoculars in the distance in the desert behind some brush. He watches Craig drive off and looks for anyone else who might be staking out the location.

Craig drives about a mile up the road and parks. Axel sees him, but isn't worried to confront Craig alone. So Axel gets in his car (actually it's Megan's car) and drives to the billboard.

Nobody else is around the billboard. Axel opens the bag Craig left for him and lifts out his cherished binder. He thumbs through the pages quickly to confirm they're his pages. He searches the bag and finds a devise in a seam of the bag. He grins and throws the bag to the ground and takes only his collection.

Axel tries to phone Craig, but it goes straight to voicemail. Craig's phone doesn't work this deep in the desert. (Craig can't call the captain either).

Axel has to pass where Craig is parked to drive back to his cabin. He decides to stop for a visit – just in case Craig was thinking about following him. He pulls behind Craig's car, parks and walks towards Craig, who also steps out of his car. Axel is unarmed and doesn't feel threatened by Craig. Craig pulls his gun and aims at Axel's head. Axel holds his hands up…

Axel: "If you shoot me, Megan dies alone in the desert. You'll never find her."

Craig: "How do I know you didn't already kill her?"

Axel: "You could ask her sister."

Craig: "How do I do that?"

Axel: "Look in my trunk..."

They walk to the trunk and Axel opens it. Rachel is restrained and has tape over her mouth. She's clothed; she has a lot of blood on her clothes and on herself, and she's sweating profusely from the heat. She has tears in her eyes and is clearly terrified.

Axel (to Rachel): "Rachel… Is Megan still alive?"

Rachel nods 'yes'

Axel: "Might she bleed to death if we don't get back to her soon?"

Rachel nods 'yes'

Axel (to Craig): "Craig, would you like to arrest me, or should I go get Megan some medical attention?"

Craig: "Fine!... But Rachel stays with me."

Axel: "No, the sisters are a set. I will return them together... Or no deal."

Craig (to Rachel): "Rachel, you hang in there. I promise, you'll be safe soon."

Axel closes the trunk.

Axel: "You will stay parked here for ten minutes. If I see you following me, I'll take a detour and you'll never find Megan."

Axel drives off, and Craig waits until his car is out of sight to turn on his tracking device. He waits the ten minutes so that Axel won't suspect he's being followed and starts to follow the signal. Craig eventually finds and turns onto the dirt road that leads to Axel's cabin. He's still out of sight and about ten minutes behind Axel. Craig tries to call the captain again, but still no reception.

Axel arrives at the cabin and re-secures Rachel to the bed in the back bedroom. By the far wall in that bedroom, there is a desk and chair. Axel puts his collection on this desk.

The layout is as follows: as you enter the cabin from the front door, you enter the main room that has the kitchen and the bed that Axel sleeps in. As you walk forward and through a doorway, you enter the back bedroom. The bed Rachel is in has the headboard against the middle of the wall to the left and her feet towards the middle of the room. The bathroom is through a doorway to the right, and Megan is restrained against the wall just past the bathroom door on the right wall. The desk with the fingerprint book is against the back wall in the center.

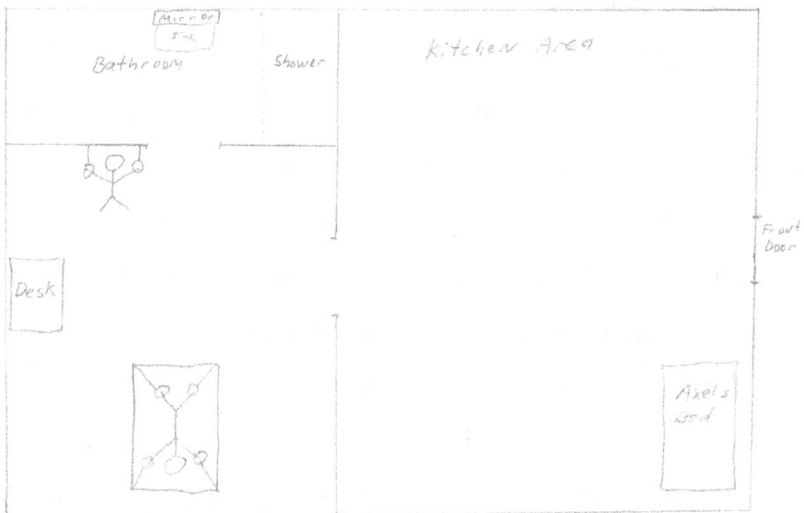

Megan is still naked and chained to the wall. She's weak from the blood loss. Axel punches her to the body a few times to weaken her even more. He uncuffs her from the wall and sits her in the chair at the desk. He then cuffs her hands behind her back, behind the back of the chair. Axel brings over a chair for himself and he opens his collection. He flips open a random page:

"See Vicky, this is Claire. I met her in Texas. She was a lot of fun for several hours. See the picture while she is alive: piercing green eyes, pretty smile. She had no idea what I was planning for her yet. She was just a slut looking for a good time. I was charged with raping her, but the sex was consensual... Then this picture is after I decapitated her with a hacksaw. I sawed her neck slow. She was alive at least 20 seconds after I started cutting. But it took at least a full minute after the screams stopped to saw through the rest of her neck... And you see a beautiful set of her fingerprints."

Megan was woozy from her injury and the blood loss, and this picture made her vomit a little onto the floor.

Axel flips some more pages, "…And this is Allison. I met her in Colorado. We fucked standing up facing each other. The sex was great. I didn't use any tools on her to kill her… like with you. When I was about to cum, I gently brought my hands to her face, brought her in for a kiss, and after the kiss, I twisted her head clockwise with both hands. There was a bone snapping sound and she started to fall. I caught her and held her up and pumped into her a few last times and I finished cumming inside her... I did have to use a knife to her right tit to get these prints though."

Axel flips ahead some more pages, "And this is Naomi, one of my first victims in LA. She was only 18. I kept her for a couple days. We made love three times. Each time, she lost a hand or a foot... Very photogenic. Her father was the one who punched me in court. I probably deserved that… And again, a good set of fingerprints."

Axel flips to the first page, "Vicky... Ah Vicky… Here's your drivers license, and a newspaper article with a black and white picture… I have all this documentation for all of my victims… But I don't have fingerprints or proper photographs for you in my collection … … not yet."

Axel stands and pulls out his Polaroid camera and takes Megan's picture. Megan is very weak and terrified. Rachel is crying on the bed.

Axel gets the large knife he'd been sharpening and rests it on the desk. He forcefully grabs Megan at the shoulder with one hand, and by the chain of the handcuffs with his other hand. He lifts and pushes Megan over the desk so that her upper body is lying face down on the desk, right next to his binder that is still open to Vicky's page. Megan is bent over at the waist. Axel holds the chain of the cuffs with his left hand so that Megan's hands are completely restrained at about the center of her back, and Axel holds her down with this hand using his weight. Axel unzips his pants and this causes a whole new panic from Megan. She can't move her upper body at all, but she starts kicking and squirming with her legs. But Axel is too close behind her, so she can't kick him. This struggling has Axel rock hard, and soon Axel is forcing himself inside her. He moves the cold knife blade against Megan's throat as he fucks her. Megan cries and screams as she's being raped.

Several minutes after this rape begins, Craig can see Axel's cabin in the distance. He had followed the tracking device to within about 300 yards of the signal and hiked the rest of the way. As he gets closer to the cabin, he hears Megan's screams and he runs faster. He knows she's being tortured or raped as he hears her cries. No time to drive back for back-up. Craig carefully approaches the front door...

Axel is so involved in his fantasy, he's able to cum without hurting Megan further. He wants to keep her around for a while. He needs this replacement for Vicky, so he doesn't want to kill her now.

Megan is weeping hard as Axel cums deep inside her pussy and hold himself inside her...

At this same moment, Craig grasps the handle of the front door of the cabin... It's unlocked.

Craig enters with his gun drawn, and from the front room, he sees Axel in the back bedroom through the doorway. Axel has his back to Craig as he's still inside Megan, but Axel quickly turns as he hears the front door open. Axel keeps the knife to Megan's throat with his right hand and lifts her to a standing position with his right forearm. He's still controlling her hands with his left hand on the handcuff's chain. This pressure on her wounded arm causes her a lot of pain; she can't fight him. Axel turns Megan so that she's between himself and Craig.

Craig sees his partner, naked; her face and body are bloody, and he sees the gunshot wound to her arm. He knows she's been through hell. As he walks toward the bedroom doorway, Craig also sees part of Rachel restrained on the bed and Axel's binder on the desk. Craig does not have a clear shot at Axel.

Craig's surprise appearance has ruined the mood for Axel, and Axel Junior goes limp and falls out of Megan. Axel retains control of Megan by her cuffs and momentarily moves the knife from her throat to re-zip his pants. And then he moves the knife back to her throat.

Axel yells, "Come any closer and I cut her throat."

Craig stays in the middle of the front room, about 25 feet away from Axel.

Craig yells with his gun pointed at Axel, "Axel… It's over… Let Megan go… Put your hands up!"

Axel replies, "It ain't over. This is just beginning…"

Axel digs the point of the knife into Megan's throat just a millimeter to bring out a tiny bit of blood to demonstrate how serious he is.

Axel begins to taunt, "Craig, you ever tap this? Her pussy is goooood."

Axel continues to use Megan as a shield. He guides her across the room so that he can get to his gun. Craig watches but is unable to safely fire a shot without endangering Megan. Axel puts down his knife and picks up his gun and points at Craig. Axel fires twice. Craig jumps to his right and takes cover by approaching and crouching next to the right side of the bedroom doorway.

But one of Axel's shots had hit Craig in his right shoulder – Craig is right handed. He'll have to hold his gun in his left hand now.

Craig peaks his head to look inside for a shot, but every time he does, Axel fires at him and Craig retreats behind the doorway.

Axel sits Megan back down at the desk. Her arms are still handcuffed behind her back and her face rests down on the desk. She isn't going anywhere.

Axel decides to draw Craig out. He takes cover behind Rachel. He kneels beside her bed so that her body is between himself and Craig. Axel removes the tape that's been covering her mouth and fires his gun into her left leg. She screams loudly in pain. Axel puts the gun to her head and says to Craig, "Throw over your gun, or I'll kill her."

Craig peaks in and sees the gun at Rachel's head and that Axel is blocked by her body. He doesn't have a shot at him. Craig retorts, "If I throw over my gun, you'll kill all three of us... How about you let the girls go and then I'll give you my gun?"

Axel replies, "You're quite the hero, but once the girls are gone, why would you give up your gun? ... This would be a stalemate, but I have two hostages I can kill... you have nothing I want... Throw over your gun, or I kill her now." Axel makes the gun 'click' as he cocks it.

Craig yells, "Megan, get away from the desk!"

Megan gathers as much energy as she can and clumsily dashes the opposite direction of Axel, toward the bathroom. Her arms, still handcuffed behind her back, knock over the chair, and she falls to the ground before she can get inside the bathroom. She is still in direct fire if Axel decides to shoot her from the other side of the room.

Craig takes a couple shots toward Axel's prized fingerprint collection on the desk. He misses a little high. Axel is clearly disturbed by this, and it gives Megan a chance to get the rest of the way into the bathroom. She hides behind the wall that's between herself and Axel, but she doesn't close the door. She can still see the doorway where Craig is.

Craig says, "You have hostages, but I think I can destroy something you cherish…"

Craig takes another couple shots at the binder, but on the third shot, there is no fire, just a click… click. Craig's gun is jammed. He doesn't have another gun. He retreats behind the right side of the doorway.

Axel stands victorious with his gun pointed at the doorway that Craig is hiding behind. Axel walks to the desk to retrieve his binder, picks it up with his left hand, and holds it to his waist.

Axel keeps the gun pointed at the doorway and calls out, "Come out Craig! …I kill Rachel in three… two…"

Craig steps into plain sight at the doorway with his hands out at his sides about a foot from his hips and says, "Axel, you win… I surrender."

Craig tosses his jammed gun to the floor. His shoulder is bleeding and Craig appears to not have any fight left in him.

Axel keeps his gun aimed at Craig, and has to gloat first, "Don't feel bad Craig. Not everyone is cut out to be a hero."

Then Axel sees that Craig has a small device in his hand… Craig presses the detonator with his thumb and the binder at Axel's waist goes 'BOOM'.

Craig recalls part of his earlier conversation with the captain after he had given him the tracking devices:

Captain: "And here's a tiny explosive, also small enough to plant within the pages of the binder. It's small, but if you detonate it while he's in his car, it is powerful enough to blow up the entire car. The detonator will work up to a mile away, but you can't blow Axel up until you find out where the girls are."

A quarter of the room is completely destroyed. The desk is in pieces and there's a gaping hole in the wall above the desk. Axel is splattered about the room. His legs are to the right of where he was standing. His arm, with the gun still in his hand, is by the bathroom door. His upper torso and head landed clear across the room by Craig at the front doorway. The middle of his body is indiscernible.

Shreds of pages of pictures and blood fingerprints are all over the room and still in the air, falling to the floor like confetti.

Megan crawls out of the bathroom, now with tears of relief. She and Craig approach Rachel on the bed. Rachel is in a state of shock from her injury. The blast ripped apart the bottom left quarter of the bed, and her foot was blown off above her ankle.

Craig unlocks Rachel's three remaining restraints and applies a tourniquet to Rachel's leg. All three of them are badly wounded, but they live another day.

They all get into Megan's car that Axel had parked just outside, and Craig drives to the closest hospital – about an hour away. A team of police are dispatched to the cabin to sort out the mess. Forensics bag up everything, including the pieces of Axel's body. They find the grave and retrieve Amy and Jenny's bodies. They find and analyze many blood stains. The blood matches Axel and Craig and Amy and Jenny and Megan and Rachel... and a woman that's been missing for ten years, last seen in Atlantic City, New Jersey.

One last thing you should know about Megan... She's pro-life... She doesn't believe in abortions...

www.ingramcontent.com/pod-product-compliance
Lightning Source LLC
Chambersburg PA
CBHW051132020726
47501CB00005B/1478